"You and I have a lot of unfinished business between us."

Ryan said the words quietly, but they still disturbed her.

"There's nothing—*nothing* between us!" Anna made a move to get to her feet, get away from him, but a warning flash from those blue eyes had her sinking back into her seat again, her legs suddenly too weak to support her.

"But there was once," he murmured, silkily.

"And you plan to tell Marc all about it!" Anna's voice was high and uneven with fear.

"Not necessarily...."

Anna's precarious grip on her self-control snapped completely. Ever since the night of the ball, Ryan had been playing with her cruelly, in the way a cat played with a mouse. "Just what is it you're after? What exactly do you want from me?"

Kate Walker chose the Brontë sisters, the development of their writing from childhood to maturity, as the topic for her master's thesis. It is little wonder, then, that she should go on to write romance fiction. She lives in the United Kingdom with her husband and son, and when she isn't writing, she tries to keep up with her hobbies of embroidery, knitting, collecting antiques and, of course, reading.

Books by Kate Walker

HARLEQUIN ROMANCE

2910—CAPTIVE LOVER
2929—MAN OF SHADOWS
2957—THE CINDERELLA TRAP
3078—JESTER'S GIRL
3107—THE GOLDEN GIRL
3174—GIVE AND TAKE

HARLEQUIN PRESENTS

1053—BROKEN SILENCE
1196—CHASE THE DAWN
1269—LEAP IN THE DARK
1374—RUNAWAY

NO GENTLEMAN
Kate Walker

Harlequin Books

TORONTO • NEW YORK • LONDON
AMSTERDAM • PARIS • SYDNEY • HAMBURG
STOCKHOLM • ATHENS • TOKYO • MILAN
MADRID • WARSAW • BUDAPEST • AUCKLAND

For Sonja and Richard

Original hardcover edition published in 1992
by Mills & Boon Limited

ISBN 0-373-03245-5

Harlequin Romance first edition January 1993

NO GENTLEMAN

CHAPTER ONE

'SO THAT'S what he looks like!'

Sonia held the glossy magazine she had been reading out at arm's length, her head tilted slightly to one side as she considered a full-page black and white photograph, her mouth pursed in a way that expressed thoughtful interest combined with sensual appreciation.

'Well, I never expected that the new golden boy of the art world would be so...' She paused, hunting for the right word. 'So rakish! I mean, look at him, Anna——'

Turning the magazine, she thrust it under the nose of the girl sitting beside her on the huge black settee.

'Isn't he the wild Irish rover personified?'

Anna didn't want to look. She thought she knew exactly what she would see if she did, and she felt as if her mind had closed up, shutting itself off from memories she had no desire to recall.

But Sonia was determined, and there was no avoiding the magazine that was only inches away from her face. Reluctantly, Anna reached for it and made a pretence of studying the photograph, resting the magazine on her knee so that her shoulder-length mane of waving blonde hair fell forward over her face as she looked down at it, hiding the disturbed expression she was unable to suppress.

For several long, taut moments, her eyes wouldn't focus, so that the picture was just a blur, and she was strongly tempted to leave it at that, hand back the magazine with some non-committal murmur, knowing she would feel more comfortable that way. But Sonia would expect a more definite reaction than that, and avoiding the facts was a coward's way out, she told herself reprovingly. What harm could a *photograph* do to her?

Blinking hard to clear her vision, she forced herself to study the photograph and found that from the moment her eyes met the arrogant, disdainful stare of its subject her gaze was held transfixed as a million disjointed thoughts surfaced inside her head.

So this was what Ryan Cassidy had become. Once more her vision blurred as memory superimposed another, more familiar image over the one on the page—the image of a dark, tough-looking youth with shaggy overlong hair that fell forward over a high forehead, carved cheekbones and a long, narrow mouth.

'Not quite the David Hockney type.' Sonia's voice intruded into her disturbed thoughts.

'He's a *portrait* painter.'

The sharp note in Anna's voice was too revealing, betraying her inner turmoil so that she regretted it at once and turned worried green eyes towards her friend. But to her relief Sonia simply shrugged smilingly.

'Does that make any difference? I thought all artists were airy-fairy types—or just plain weird. But then you know me—thick as a plank when it comes to cultural matters. But I do know a man when I see one, and that character is definitely male with a capital M. I wonder if he gives art lessons,' she went on thoughtfully, with another appreciative glance at the photograph.

Anna gave a weak snort of laughter.

'The man who's been hailed as the greatest portrait painter of the decade and who's the bookmakers' favourite to be commissioned to paint the Prince and Princess of Wales doesn't need to take students to to up his income. Besides, your Mr Cassidy's too much in demand to have time for unimportant things like helping struggling amateurs.'

This time, the tartness of her tone penetrated the sensual fantasy that had filled Sonia's head ever since she had first seen the photograph, and she turned a frankly curious gaze on her friend.

'You seem to have a very low opinion of the man,' she declared, surprise lifting her voice. 'When did he tread on your toes, then?'

'He didn't!'

Anna blurted out the words far too quickly, uncomfortably aware of the way that the barriers she kept between her present life and her past had weakened dangerously.

'I—was thinking of his reputation. For a start, I'm surprised that he ever gave that interview—after all, isn't "difficult" the word most often used to describe him? And he's supposed to be *very* particular whom he chooses to accept as a subject for his talents——'

One slim hand gestured towards the headline that topped the article that accompanied the photograph. 'The Man Money Can't Buy' it read in bold, dark print.

'You can't have forgotten how he earned that particular nickname.'

Sonia's laugh revealed that she remembered the incident very well indeed.

'You mean when Drew Curtiss tried to commission him to paint a portrait of his wife—his fourth, wasn't she? And at least a quarter of a century younger than him.'

She didn't need Anna's silent nod of confirmation, being deeply involved in her own reminiscence, a smile of amusement curving her lips at the thought of the response the artist had given to the millionaire industrialist.

'Cassidy refused categorically—and went on refusing even when Drew offered more and more money. I don't know what the final figure was—I heard it was hundreds of thousands—but it was turned down like all the rest.'

'With the declaration that Cassidy had better things to do,' Anna put in wryly.

'And wasn't Drew furious when those "better things" turned out to be just a series of paintings of down-and-outs on the streets of Manchester—for which Cassidy wasn't paid a penny? Mmm, yes, he's nobody's puppet, that's for sure,' Sonia said, a note in her voice suggesting that that was a trait she found very appealing. 'Hey—you don't think he'd turn down the Royals, do you?'

'I don't know.' Anna couldn't resist a gentle tease. 'I wouldn't put it past him.'

'But wouldn't that be treason or something? I mean, can you refuse a royal command?'

'*Joke*, Sonia,' Anna put in hastily, but as she spoke her eyes slid back to the picture in the magazine and her voice faltered slightly. The Ryan Cassidy she had known would have been quite capable of turning down a commission from God himself. He had never given a damn about anyone but himself—or perhaps his older brother.

A dark shadow of sorrow clouded Anna's widely spaced moss-green eyes at the thought of Larry. It didn't seem possible that he had been dead for almost eight years now. He had been just twenty-seven, her own age now, which meant that Ryan must be thirty or thirty-one. Secretly, Anna studied the photograph before her for some sign of a family likeness.

But there was no resemblance there, except, perhaps, in the wide mouth, and even that was so very different because one of the things she remembered about Larry was that he had always been smiling. *This* Cassidy looked as if he never smiled, his mouth just a hard, straight line, and the bold, unwavering, arrogant stare made him look as if he had just told the photographer to go to hell instead of agreeing to the pose, which Anna felt must have been carefully set up to present exactly the right image.

The black hair and strongly carved features had been caught perfectly in black and white, but one thing that the photograph couldn't show was the stunning colour of his eyes, those amazing, clear, vivid blue eyes fringed with heavy black lashes, their intensity of colour almost shocking against the harsh lines of his face and the raven's-wing colour of his hair. They were what she remembered when she thought of Ryan Cassidy—something she had been doing a lot lately, ever since reports of the way he had abandoned his seclusion in the north and come to London had spread through the newspapers and magazines. Before that, busy with her own life, she would have said that she had forgotten that he had ever existed, though that was not strictly true. Ryan Cassidy, and the part he had played in her life, was carefully locked away in her own private Pandora's box of memories, never to be opened, she had thought, until the prospect of his arrival in London, in her new world, had flung the lid wide.

But then she had never expected to hear of him again. She had certainly not dreamed that she would read of him in the pages of a glossy magazine like the one Sonia was now studying once more, reading the article which accompanied the photograph.

'He's an interesting character by all accounts,' she murmured, her eyes fixed on the print. 'No formal training—he's just built his reputation by word of mouth, and—hey, Anna—he's from your part of the country— up north.'

As usual, Sonia gave the last two words an exagger-
atedly accented intonation that was her idea of Yorkshire
pronunciation, turning the 'up' into 'oop'.

'He grew up in the Churtown district of Forgeley.'

She glanced up, her eyes bright with curiosity.

'What's that like?'

'Rough,' Anna declared succinctly, giving the description a forceful, disparaging emphasis, and saw
Sonia's eyebrows fly up in response so that for a moment
she was gripped with a sense of panic at the thought that
perhaps she had gone too far, made too much of her
disapproval.

'So he's dragged himself up by his bootstraps, then.'
Once more that note of sensuality touched Sonia's voice.
'A real rough diamond. Did you ever know of him
when——?'

Anna decided that that particular line of questioning
was best broken off as quickly—and as non-committally
as possible.

'Yorkshire's a huge county, Anna—and Forgeley a
large city in it.'

'Yes, I suppose it is,' Sonia, whose knowledge of the
geography of the United Kingdom ended north of
Watford, agreed thoughtfully. 'And of course you and
Cassidy will have moved in very different circles. You
know, perhaps one day we should all go on an ex-
pedition to Yorkshire—back to your roots.'

She made it sound like a trek to the outback, Anna
reflected, which, to Sonia, it probably was. The sudden
quiver of fear in the pit of her stomach unnerved her.
It was over two years since she had felt this threatened
by the mention of her past—with both her parents dead
and no other family, she had thought that the carefully
edited version of her story which she had given her
friends would never be challenged. But now, experi-

encing the sense of panic which had assailed her in the past, she couldn't avoid connecting it with Sonia's interest in Ryan Cassidy, and it made her distinctly uneasy.

'I don't know when I'll have time to fit that in,' she replied carefully, not wanting to alert her friend's suspicions any more than she already had. 'Things are pretty hectic at the moment, and you know how difficult it would be to drag Marc away. In the three years I've known your brother he hasn't taken a single day's holiday——.'

'Well, surely now that you two are going to be partners you should be able to persuade him to have some time off.'

'It's just a business arrangement!' Anna declared hastily, flustered by the deliberate emphasis Sonia had put on the word 'partners'. The look her friend gave her was frankly sceptical.

'You know Marc—it's always business *first*,' she said pointedly, with an arch smile. 'And I don't think it's just shares in Nature's Secrets he's after.'

Just at that moment the door opened and the subject of their conversation strolled into the room. Immediately Anna's heart lifted, a glow lighting in her eyes as her gaze went to Marc Denton's smoothly handsome face, and she pushed her earlier disturbed thoughts to the back of her mind. Ryan Cassidy was the past; Marc was the most important part of her present—and, hopefully, if Sonia's none too subtle hints were to be believed, of her future too.

Was it possible that he was planning on extending their new business partnership in her natural cosmetics company into another, much more personal form of commitment? Mrs Marc Denton. In the privacy of her thoughts she let herself try out the sound of the name that might one day be hers, letting it linger delightfully in her mind. Would she be foolish to allow herself to hope? Ever since she had left Empire Street to build a new life for herself she had dreamed of just such a moment, and for months now she had known that Marc was the man with whom she wanted to spend that future.

But her determination to leave her past behind her meant that she had never told Marc, or anyone she had met since, the truth about her earlier life. For the first time since she had taken it, Anna was forced to consider the wisdom of the decision she had made years before.

'We'd almost given you up—Anna and I were about to go on to the restaurant by ourselves.'

'I got held up.' Marc brushed a light kiss on Anna's forehead before he sank down on to a chair. 'Sorry.'

The apology was offered automatically, with no real sense of regret behind it. Marc Denton was a man whose life revolved around his work, and his family and friends all knew that.

'Hard day?' Anna asked, as Marc stretched luxuriously.

'Satisfying,' he returned laconically. 'But that isn't why I'm late—I met Gillie Ford, and she wanted to talk about a charity do she's organising.'

Sonia made a sound that was halfway between a groan and a laugh.

'Gillie and her good deeds! What is it this time? Save the ozone layer or free battery hens—chicken's lib?'

'An arts centre for deprived kids. Somewhere where they can do something constructive: painting, woodwork, weaving, embroidery—any sort of craft— instead of hanging around on street corners.'

'I think that's a wonderful idea!' Anna put in abruptly, her private thoughts making her tone rather more emphatic than she had intended, causing Marc to look at her in some surprise. If there had been some such centre in Forgeley when she had lived there, then perhaps life would not have been quite so miserable. Surely her father would have let her go there, meet other young people under supervision, and she wouldn't have felt so appallingly isolated. 'I think it could work very well,' she added awkwardly.

'You're probably right. At least it should have a little more practical effect than some of Gillie's schemes. You have to admit that she can be pretty hare-brained at times. Anyway, she's holding a ball cum—to quote Gillie—"cultural extravaganza" to raise funds for the project.'

'Cultural extravaganza?' Sonia echoed the words curiously. 'What on earth's that?'

'She's inviting everyone she knows in the art world—designers, painters, sculptors—to contribute prizes for a huge raffle which she plans to draw on the night of the ball.'

A feeling like the fluttering of the wings of a dozen trapped birds started up inside Anna's stomach as her mind caught on a particular word in Marc's reply and emphasised it with a painfully sharp focus so that the rest of what he had to say was just a blur.

Painters. After the conversation she had just had with Sonia, her thoughts naturally centred on one painter in particular and a cold, creeping fear gripped her. Would Ryan Cassidy be invited to contribute to Gillie's 'cultural extravaganza', and, if so, would he be at the ball?

'So of course I said we'd go along.' Luckily, absorbed in his monologue, Marc hadn't noticed Anna's temporary abstraction. 'Some of Gillie's schemes may be half-baked, but she always does things with style, and you can guarantee that anyone who is anyone will be there.'

Anna's eyes went to Marc, lingering on his clean-cut features, the cold sense of fear seeming to reach her heart as her mind repeated his last words and she faced the thought that this was precisely why she had never told him the truth about her life before she had met him. At first she had been unable even to think the words Empire Street, and later, when she had got to know Marc better, she had realised that to reveal her past had a new and different sort of danger.

If there was one thing that concerned Sonia's brother more than his work it was his standing in society; he would never countenance anything which might sully his carefully cultivated position as someone who 'was' someone. If he were ever to find out that her background was not the comfortably off, cultured one she had led him to believe in, it was most likely that she could say goodbye to those rosy dreams of a future as his wife which she had just allowed herself to admit meant so much to her.

'Perfect!' Sonia's smile was one of pure delight. 'I've been looking for an excuse to get something new. Anna, you and I must go shopping together—find something absolutely gorgeous and dramatic.'

Anna managed a non-committal murmur which her friend could take any way she wanted. For one thing, Sonia had a taste for frills and flounces while Anna herself preferred a more simple, tailored way of dressing, like the beige linen suit she was wearing now, one which looked better on her slim five-foot-eight inch frame. Privately, she envied her friend her curves, feeling that her own shape was far too boyishly slender to be truly feminine.

And 'dramatic' might fit Sonia with her blue-black hair and dark, flashing eyes, but such a description could never be applied to her own colouring. For one thing, her skin was too pale, and, particularly in an unexpectedly hot summer such as this, unflatteringly disposed to freckles.

Once more Anna's thoughts went to the memories of Larry Cassidy, which the sight of his brother's photograph had so recently re-awoken. As a teenager, people had sometimes taken her and Larry for brother and sister, not connecting Ryan with him at all. Larry had had the true rich copper hair and green eyes that were associated in people's minds with his Celtic ancestry—his mother and father both coming from Ireland. In Anna, that colouring was muted, her eyes, widely spaced in a narrow face, the soft, deep colour of moss, her hair a deep gold shot through with strands of copper so that the whole effect was of a tawny colour, not blonde, not red, but a mixture of the two.

'I'm sure my blue——' she said slowly.

'Oh, Anna, no! You can't wear that *again*. Everyone's seen it——'

'Actually, Gillie planned on making it a fancy-dress ball,' Marc put in, his frown of distaste revealing that the idea was not one which appealed to him personally. 'So you'll have to hire a costume anyway.'

His comment diverted Sonia on to a different track and, as she debated the different costumes she might choose, Anna gave a small private sigh of relief at the fact that the topic of designer dresses had been dropped. The deeply ingrained habits of thrift which had dominated the majority of her life died hard, and, although she was by no means poor, the casual way Sonia spoke of spending large amounts of money was a constant reminder of how hard she had worked to get this far, how she might still be struggling with her tiny business if it hadn't been for Marc.

But perhaps now, if Sonia was right about her brother's intentions, she really could put those days of penny-pinching and unhappiness well behind her—forever.

This was her world now, Anna thought some hours later, looking at the scene in the exclusive restaurant as if from the outside, seeing herself and her companions as others might see them. This was where she belonged, the life she had worked so hard to achieve. Memories of Ryan Cassidy or any part of Empire Street had no place in this world, and she had no intention of letting the man who had once darkened her past cast a black shadow over what she had gained.

With Marc she could find the security and stability that had been lacking in so much of the rest of her life. If she did become Mrs Marc Denton then that really would be one in the eye for Ryan Cassidy and his type. And perhaps, after all, she had worried unnecessarily. Surely if Mark wanted to marry her—if he loved her—then he wouldn't mind about her past, knowing that it was their future together which mattered.

So it was with a light heart that Anna left the restaurant and walked with Marc to where he had parked his car, Sonia having opted to go on to a nightclub, where she was meeting her latest boyfriend. Her mind still full of her high hopes for the future, she was shocked when the quiet of the night was shattered by a piercing wolf-whistle.

'Hey, gorgeous!' The shout, like the whistle, came from behind them. 'Give us a kiss!'

There was nothing threatening in the man's voice, and, besides, Marc was with her; she was quite safe. But, with thoughts of Ryan Cassidy and Empire Street still lingering in her mind, Anna froze in shock, her mind slipping back over the years so that she felt as if she were fifteen again, lost and terribly afraid.

Immediately Marc swung round, his movement taking Anna with him as he hadn't released her hand.

'Now look here, you lout!'

'I'd rather look at the lady,' was the slurred response. 'How about it, darlin'? How 'bout a kiss for a bloke on his last night of freedom?'

'So this is where you are!'

Another voice sounded out of the darkness of the car park, a voice that made Anna's breath catch in her throat as she caught the faint traces of an Irish lilt in its northern-accented deep tones. She had heard hundreds, thousands of voices in the years since she had left Empire Street, some of them accented like this one, but this voice went straight to her heart like an arrow thudding into the gold in the centre of the target so that she knew that the second man could be no other than Ryan Cassidy himself.

'What are you up to now? Get into the car, you idiot!'

'Get into the car.' If Anna had had any doubts before, there were none in her mind now. Those four simple words, an ordinary, everyday phrase, had started it all and, spoken in this particular voice, they seemed to burn into her brain as if formed in letters of fire.

'I'm sorry about this.' The apology was flung in Anna's and Marc's direction, a hint of laughter behind the words implying that he felt it was quite unnecessary, as he bundled his inebriated companion into the car before moving round to the driver's seat himself. 'It's been quite a night.'

A few moments later, the dark sports car sped past them on the way towards the exit and as Anna watched it go by her numbed mind registered vaguely the fact that its sleek lines and powerful engine were in sharp

contrast to the battered wreck he had driven on tha
fateful night all those years before. Then Marc's dis
gusted exclamation made her look more closely, catching
a brief glimpse of the figure in the passenger-seat, who
had turned and was blowing extravagant kisses in her
direction.

'Bloody louts!'

Marc's angry exclamation brought her eyes to his face
her heart sinking immediately, her earlier euphoric mood
evaporating swiftly to be replaced by the cold, sickening
ache of fear as she saw the dark fury and disgust tha
suffused his face.

'Back-street northern yobs! Probably down here fo
some football match. They're not fit to be with civilise
people!'

The cold ache grew worse, and Anna felt as if an ic
hand was gripping her heart. Unlike herself, Marc ha
no earlier knowledge on which to judge the men they
had just encountered. All it had taken was the sound o
a northern accent and they had been assessed, judged
and categorised as the sort of louts who were beneat
his contempt. The fact that she knew that, for Ryan
Cassidy at least, that description was fully justified
didn't make things any easier. All she could think of wa
that Marc would never be able to accept the fact tha
she came from the same town—the same street—as the
men he had just dismissed out of hand.

'Last night of freedom indeed!'

The rest of Marc's angry mutter faded, becoming in
audible, as a shiver shook Anna's body. Only now did
the phrase Cassidy's companion had used hit home fully
making her heart lurch painfully at the thought of jus
what he had meant.

'How about a kiss for a bloke on his last night o
freedom?' he had said, and his voice had been shaded

by the same Irish lilt as Ryan's, which probably meant that he had been Rory, the middle Cassidy son—Ryan's disreputable brother.

In the past, Rory wasn't someone she had taken too much notice of. From the first, she had had eyes only for Larry, and at that time Rory had been running wild with a rough pack of youths who had shocked her father and terrified Anna herself.

Then, later, at the time of Larry's funeral, Rory had been what was euphemistically referred to as 'away'—in other words, in prison, serving a sentence for burglary. No one had expected Ryan to appear either; he had been missing for almost three years by then, and no one, except perhaps his mother, had the faintest idea where he had gone. But he *had* turned up, and the repercussions of that unexpected visit had had devastating effects on Anna's life. The events of that single day had been the final straw which had pushed her to breaking-point and made her vow to start a new life for herself.

Anna shivered again, feeling cold through to her bones in spite of the warm summer night. She could only be grateful that Marc was too concerned with his own annoyance at the brief scene to question her about her silence. If he had said anything she wouldn't have known how to answer him, couldn't have found the words to explain the shaken reaction which she knew would show in her voice without revealing the sordid details of the past which she had always kept so carefully hidden from him.

So Rory Cassidy was back in circulation again—but not for long, it seemed. The youthful tearaway hadn't changed at all in the years since she had got away from Empire Street. His last night of freedom. What was he going to prison for this time? Burglary again, or something worse? Whatever it was, Ryan obviously wasn't too concerned by his brother's unlawful behaviour—the tolerant amusement in his voice had shown that only too clearly.

Ryan Cassidy. The feeling of hope, the sense of joy she had known earlier in the evening had vanished completely, leaving Anna feeling as limp as a damp rag. It all came back to him, as it had done all those years before.

The car he drove might be very different; he might be the toast of the art world, its new rising star, with the income to go with his status, but underneath the surface glamour he was still the rough, dangerous lout he had always been—the sort of man she had left Forgeley to get away from and had hoped never to have to face again.

And, knowing how Marc felt about his position in society, his reputation, and that of anyone closely connected with him, she could only curse the terrible irony of fate that had made their paths cross again now, when it seemed that she was about to take the final step away from Empire Street and all that it had meant.

'You know Marc—it's always business *first*,' Sonia had said, and Anna knew that was true. Even in marriage Marc Denton would always consider the pros and cons very carefully.

He would want his future wife to be an asset to him. The woman he married would have to be beyond reproach, and Ryan Cassidy was the one man who, with a few careless words, could destroy her life as totally now as he had done once before in the past—more so probably, because this time she had so much more to lose.

CHAPTER TWO

'ISN'T this fun?' Sonia, her face slightly flushed from the heat under the elaborate make-up Anna had created to go with her Cleopatra costume, sank down on a chair beside her friend. 'Gillie's certainly done us proud this time.'

Anna nodded agreement, looking out at the crowded, beautifully decorated ballroom, crammed with men and women in every possible costume imaginable. Close to her, a red devil danced with an angel, a gorilla with a scantily clad Peter Pan. There were kings and queens, a black cat, Father Christmas, and even a medieval knight, who must be extremely uncomfortable and hot in his suit of armour—but luckily for her peace of mind, so far at least, there had been no sign of the tall frame, black hair and gypsyish dark looks of Ryan Cassidy.

'Where's Marc?'

'Gone to get some champagne.'

'Wonderful! I could kill for a drink; I've been dancing non-stop for over an hour.'

With a contented sigh, Sonia stretched her legs out in front of her, admiring her feet in the ornately jewelled sandals.

'William's gone to join the queue to get some raffle tickets,' she went on. 'I've been trying to get Gillie to let me in on the secret of the mystery prize but she's giving nothing away. She simply looked smug and said that what was in the envelope was the first prize—so it has to be something rather special. Have you any ideas?'

'None at all,' Anna responded, recalling how she had paused by the table on which the raffle prizes were laid out, noting with some satisfaction the way that her own contribution of a huge gift set of Nature's Secrets products, their clear glass bottles elegantly arranged in a white-satin-lined box, had been prominently displayed well to the front. It was only as she was about to move away that her eye had been caught by an item that looked decidedly out of place among the other luxurious items. At the very back of the table, pinned to a display board, was an ordinary brown manila envelope emblazoned with a large red question mark. 'But you're probably right—it will be something spectacular.'

'And while we're talking of spectacular things,' Sonia put in, a smile on her face, 'I told you that costume would be perfect—Marc's eyes were out on stalks when he saw you.'

'Hardly,' Anna demurred. Marc wasn't that sort of man; he kept his feelings very much to himself. But all the same she knew that the dress she was wearing suited her perfectly.

In soft white silk, it was Regency in design, the sort of dress that might have been worn by a Jane Austen heroine, and indeed the costume hire shop owner had said that it was one of a pair: the costumes for Elizabeth Bennett and Mr Darcy in a recent production of *Pride and Prejudice*. On someone else, its simplicity might have looked too plain, almost drab, and yet on Anna it had a stunning sort of impact. Its delicate colour contrasted sharply with her hair, making it gleam like burnished gold, turning her eyes into deep forest pools, dark and mysterious. The tiny puffed sleeves exposed the slenderness of her arms, and the high waistline, fitting just underneath her breasts, softened the angularity of her figure so that the low, scooped neckline suggested at a cleavage, something she had never known in her life before. When she moved the skirt swung around her ankles like a soft cloud, and the delicate satin slippers which the hire shop had provided were so light on her feet that she felt as if she was walking on air.

Anna waved the gold and white fan, which, with last-minute inspiration, she had added as an accessory to her outfit, in an attempt to cool her flushed cheeks.

'I wish Marc would hurry up with the drinks. It's so hot in here.'

'I'll bet he'll be ages yet—he's probably met some business cronies and is deep in a discussion of the vagaries of the stock market. Look, why don't you go outside and get a breath of fresh air? I'll tell Marc where you've gone—*when* he turns up.'

'I think I'll do that.' Anna got to her feet. 'Five minutes outside should refresh me—I'll be back in time for supper.'

She made slow progress towards the open french doors out into the garden, the short journey one of stops and starts and changes of direction necessary to avoid the brightly dressed men and women who milled about her, and, never one to like large gatherings, preferring quiet, intimate meetings with a few friends, she found that by the time she finally achieved her objective she was feeling distinctly frayed, and she stepped out into the quiet of the garden with a sigh of relief.

Even though it was now fully dark, except where the light from the ballroom spilled out over the lawns, it was still very warm, the night carrying the scent of hundreds of flowers that hung on the air like a soft perfume. Her satin slippers making no sound, Anna wandered down the path, feeling some of her tension ease as she drew in long, deep breaths of the night air.

She had vowed that she wouldn't think of such things tonight, but she couldn't stop her thoughts from going back to the times when Marc had first invited her to events like this and she had often felt the need to escape, get away for a few minutes to relax from the strain of being in such a totally different world from the one she had known. Perhaps because it was the world to which she very much wanted to belong, she had been terrified of putting a foot wrong, showing herself up, so that she would never win acceptance. For so much of her life she had lived as an outsider, enduring the isolation of not really belonging. But now she *did* belong. She moved in the sort of society from which her father had come and to which he had always dreamed of going back. He had never made it, but she had achieved his ambition for him.

The faint sound of a footstep on the path at her back had Anna stiffening for a moment, but immediately common sense reasserted itself and she relaxed again. It was only Marc, who, having returned to their table with the drinks, had been told where she was and had come looking for her. Deliberately she slowed her pace to show that she was waiting for him, though she didn't turn to face him but kept her eyes fixed on the ornamental pond a few yards away where a tiny fountain played in its centre.

It was such a romantic setting: the garden, bathed in moonlight, the scent of flowers and the soft sound of the splashing water, and Anna's heart suddenly leapt at the thought that perhaps Marc had sought her out here for a special reason. Perhaps he had chosen tonight to propose to her. If he had she knew exactly what her answer would be. She would say yes willingly and happily. They would go back inside to announce their engagement and then surely, as the prospective Mrs Marc

Denton, she would finally feel secure in the knowledge that she would never be an outsider again.

The quiet footsteps came nearer, soft and slow, quite unlike Marc's usual brisk way of walking. Normally he strode through life as if there was no time to stop and dream. If Anna regretted that, it was only for a moment. She understood that if you wanted to get on in life you had to concentrate your energies totally on your ambitions. After all, wasn't that the way she had lived ever since the idea of Nature's Secrets had become more than a dream in her head and had turned into a definite reality?

But tonight was a moment suspended out of time. In the fantasy setting of the costume ball, in this beautiful garden, there was a chance to pause, to admit to other dreams, ones that had had to be suppressed while she had concentrated on her central aim. And perhaps Marc felt it too. Perhaps that was why he hadn't called to her, knowing that his crisp, clear tones would shatter the atmosphere irrevocably. So she kept her eyes fixed on the sparkling spray of the fountain and waited.

He was very close now. She could hear his steady breathing, could almost feel its warmth on the back of her neck where the delicate skin was exposed by the way she had pulled her hair up into a knot of curls at the top of her head. A glow of happiness washed through her like the soft touch of warm water on her skin. Never before had she and Marc been so intuitively, so emphatically in tune with each other's mood—but at that moment all rational thought fled from her mind as strong arms slid round her waist and she was pulled gently but firmly back against a hard, masculine form.

Anna's breath caught in her throat, her eyes opening wide, seeing the stars in the night sky with a new and almost painfully sharp clarity as her body responded to the warmth that surrounded her, the lean muscularity of the body that was pressed against her back, her hips, her legs, every nerve coming suddenly tinglingly alive, a sigh of delight escaping her as she felt warm lips brush the sensitive skin at the back of her neck in an infinitely gentle caress.

She didn't need to speak, didn't want him to say anything that would break the magic of the moment that enclosed them both. Never before had she been so intensely aware of his masculinity and her femininity. Never before had one tiny touch aroused such a searing sensation of need, such an aching longing to be held and caressed, to be kissed until she was senseless with passion. She felt as if her body was starting to melt, as if her legs, even the path beneath her feet, were dissolving, becoming insubstantial, so that if he released her she would sink to the ground, unable to stand alone.

Languidly she let her head drop back against one powerful shoulder, her eyes half closed, knowing a deep contentment when the dark shape of his head obscured the moon as he bent to kiss her. His mouth was confident yet sensually gentle, so unlike the brief, almost businesslike kisses he had bestowed on her before, and she responded with an unthinking eagerness, letting her lips soften under his, feeling her heart starting to race, the blood heat in her veins, so that it was as if she stood in the full heat of a summer sun and not the cool, pale light of the moon. She had never dreamed that Marc could make her feel like this.

Butterfly kisses trailed a path along the line of her throat, across her cheek, and she heard a low, husky laugh, his breath feathering warmly against her skin.

'So, my lovely,' he whispered. 'I think you were waiting for me.'

If the gentle spray from the fountain had turned into
a ferocious blast of icy water flung straight into her face,
Anna could not have been more shocked. Her head went
back as if she'd been slapped in the face, her mind reeling
as she tried to reject what she'd heard—the soft, lilting
note of an Irish accent in the voice of the man behind
her.

For a long moment she froze into immobility, still as
a statue in the circle of those enclosing arms, but then
a wave of anger and disgust drove away the stunned sense
of disbelief, giving her the strength to spin round to face
him.

'I most definitely was——'

The final 'not' wouldn't form in her mouth as her
eyes went to his face and she saw, with no hope of denial,
the full truth of what, even now, she still, irrationally,
hoped was just a trick of the dark, or a nightmare from
which she would awake to find that she had imagined
that revealing voice.

But this was no dream. She was wide awake, and there
was no way she could deny the truth of that strongly
carved, high-cheekboned face and the deep-set eyes that
gleamed in the moonlight, drained of their colour so that
they were just dark, impenetrable pools. Eyes which
could belong to no one but Ryan Cassidy.

'And I was looking for you.' That soft voice went on
as if she hadn't spoken. 'And what a perfect place to
find you—here, in the garden, with——'

'I was *not* waiting for you!'

A wave of panic brought on by the forced recognition
of the fact that his words were echoing her thoughts of
a moment before, and a deep-felt dread of hearing any
more of the idyll she had thought she'd shared with Marc
expressed by this man who epitomised everything she

hated, everything she had thought she'd escaped from, drove Anna into hasty speech.

An infuriatingly arrogant lift of one dark eyebrow questioned her declaration, making her rush on thoughtlessly.

'As a matter of fact, I thought you were my——'

A belated rush of conscience made her bite off the word she had been about to use, knowing it was not strictly true, but she knew from the way those clear eyes flicked to her left hand, now clutching the delicate fan as if it were a weapon she could use against him, that he had inserted 'fiancé' into her silence anyway.

'I thought you were someone else,' she finished lamely.

'Marcus Denton?' Ryan Cassidy supplied casually.

How did he know that? How did he know *anything* about her? Did he think that she was a stranger, or had he remembered——?

Her mind dodged away from completing that question, and the next moment she was too thoroughly disconcerted to be able to consider answering it because it was only when he released her that Anna realised that all this time she had still been in his arms because she had turned to him while still within their confining circle. She was grateful for the shadows in the darkened garden that hid the wash of colour across her face, then drew in a sharp breath as for the first time she took in the full effect of his appearance.

The epitome of the Regency dandy stood before her in a rich blue cut-away coat, white shirt and crimson waistcoat, tight-fitting breeches and highly polished riding boots, a fine cravat falling from his throat like the foam that bubbled in the fountain.

Anna found that she was disturbingly aware of the way the elegant coat fitted snugly around straight, square shoulders, the way its jacket was cut short at the front, falling into tails behind, revealing a slim waistline and narrow hips around which the skin-tight breeches clung in a way that even the most close-fitting denims never could. The silk shirt and elaborate cravat, which could have looked effeminate on another man, somehow had the effect of heightening the powerful masculinity of Cassidy's rough-hewn features, making them appear darker and more forcefully male in contrast to their delicacy. It was as if the rake in every Regency romance novel she had ever read had suddenly stepped off the page to appear, alive and infinitely disturbing, before her. And, like some swooning heroine of the same novels, she felt an almost uncontrollable urge to open her fan and wave it in front of her face to hide her blushes and cool her burning cheeks.

'I think you've made some sort of mistake,' she said, the taut state of her nerves making her voice cold and stiff.

Ryan shook his dark head firmly.

'No mistake, my lovely—and, if I had any doubts that you were who I was looking for, then you've just rid me of them once and for all.'

Fear seemed to freeze the blood in Anna's veins, and the look she turned on Ryan was equally icy, though the tension in her facial muscles, which made her look so condescendingly haughty, was put there as much by panic as by pride.

'I don't know what you mean,' she declared tightly, praying he didn't mean what she thought he did, and was frankly stunned when Ryan threw back his head and laughed out loud.

'That settles it,' he said, and Anna was unnerved to find that the laughter still lingering in his voice did nothing to warm it; instead it left a dark thread of sardonic humour running through his speech. 'I know that look of old—that "what is this disgusting smell beneath my nose?" expression.'

Abruptly and frighteningly every trace of laughter fled from his face so that it looked terrifyingly hard and bleak.

'I saw enough of that in the past to last me a lifetime—didn't I, *Anna-Louise*?'

'My name is Anna——' Anna felt as if the words might actually fall from her lips as chips of ice, they sounded so cold and proud, and the sudden flash of Ryan's eyes in the moonlight warned her that her tone had been a mistake.

'Oh, yes, I understand that's what you call yourself now—but we both know it wasn't always so, don't we, my lovely?'

'I don't know what you're talking about.'

She didn't have much hope that he would believe her, and of course he didn't, his hand coming out to grip her arm, restraining her when she would have pushed past him to head back to the ballroom.

'You know exactly what I'm talking about—just as you know very well who I am.'

Anna's heart seemed to be pounding high up in her throat, making it impossible to breathe naturally. She knew a desperate longing to turn and run, back into the ballroom, to find Marc——

Marc. Her stomach twisted into tight, painful knots of tension. By now, Marc must be wondering where she was. Her heart lurched at the thought of him finding her together with Ryan Cassidy like this.

'If you'll excuse me, I have to get back inside——'

She made a movement to shake his hand from her arm, and to her surprise Ryan released her at once, standing back as if to let her go—but she didn't like the smile that curved his lips; it was a smile of triumph, with no warmth in it at all.

'Surely if Mr Denton were concerned about you he'd have come looking for you,' he murmured silkily, making her freeze as she was about to take a step forward.

Why had he had to make that comment about Marc? In that one brief sentence he had taken her earlier happiness, the dreamlike moments she had experienced in the garden, and destroyed them as savagely as if they had been a delicate flower he had crushed under his feet. If she were honest, she knew that Marc was unlikely to come looking for her. Once he became absorbed in some discussion of investments and interest rates, he forgot about anything else.

'You've no right to say anything about Marc!' Her inner unease made the words far more forceful than she had ever intended. 'You know nothing about him!'

'I know that he's a very rich man,' Ryan returned smoothly. 'So tell me, Anna-Louise—is that the attraction—the fact that he can give you everything you want?'

'No, it isn't!' Anna denied angrily. Ryan Cassidy would never understand just what it was that Marc gave her. He had never known the need for stability and security that had haunted her younger years. 'For one thing, Marc is a gentleman, and that's something you'll never be!'

Her outburst was a mistake, she knew that as soon as she saw the way his face closed up, his eyes narrowing to mere slits in a face that was white with barely controlled anger. Her breath caught in her throat and instinctively she flinched away as Ryan made a move towards her. But Cassidy simply caught hold of her hand and held it gently.

'No gentleman,' he murmured, the softness of his tone making Anna's breath catch in her throat in surprise. 'Is that what you think of me? I'm sure, given half a chance, I could easily prove otherwise.'

Then, to Anna's astonishment and complete consternation, he performed a low, elaborate bow over her hand, pressing his lips to it lingeringly.

Her first impulse was to snatch her hand away as quickly as possible. He was just playing with her, she knew that, taking on the role of Mr Darcy that his costume suggested. But at the same time a small, unwary part of her heart in which the sense of magic she had experienced earlier still lingered was touched by the image he presented with that proud, dark head bent over her hand, and the moonlight bathing him in its pale, unearthly gleam. No one had ever bowed to her, or kissed her hand before, and she couldn't help thinking that no other man she knew, certainly not Marc, could perform the old-fashioned gesture of courtesy with the consummate grace and total lack of self-consciousness that Ryan Cassidy displayed. Acting independently of her rational mind, her pulse-rate quickened disturbingly in response to the light pressure of his fingers on hers.

But then Ryan lifted his head and smiled deep into her eyes and Anna's heart lurched suddenly as she saw the gleam of cynical amusement and challenge in their blue depths.

Immediately the spell was broken. She knew that look of old; Cassidy was no longer the romantic Mr Darcy but the man who had treated her so appallingly all those years ago, and she snatched her hand away from his warm grasp as swiftly as if she had been burned.

'It takes more than a few fancy gestures to make a gentleman, Mr Cassidy!' she declared, her voice sounding high and sharp in the still night air. 'And now, if you'll excuse me, I would much prefer to go back inside.'

'Of course——'

To Anna's horror, his hand came out to take her arm. Clearly he intended to go with her, back into the ballroom, where everyone she knew would see them together, and Marc——

'*No*!'

With a desperate cry she dragged her arm free, the force of her movement making her take several steps away from him.

'Don't touch me! I don't want you with me—Marc would——'

Her voice failed her, the words shrivelling on her tongue as she saw the savage anger that darkened Ryan's face, the terrifying flash of his eyes in the moonlight.

'Marc would——?' he echoed, his tone harshly questioning. 'Tell me, Miss Miller, what would Mr Denton do?'

'He——'

Anna couldn't find the words to answer him. Not for the first time she wished that she had had the courage to tell Marc the truth weeks ago, when the idea of the ball had first been mentioned. But, if she were honest, even then it had already been too late. The seeds of the situation in which she now found herself had been laid three years ago when she had first met Marc and, still unable even to think of Empire Street without panic, had given him a carefully edited version of her life story. He had known that she had grown up in the north but she had never dared admit to the full reality of just where.

Later, as she came to know him better, to realise the emphasis he put on his standing in the wealthy and aristocratic circles in which he moved, and as Marc himself became more important in her own life, any impulse to tell him the truth had been smothered under a rush of fear at the thought of how he would react if he were to discover how she had deceived him. The one thing she was sure of was that he would never, ever accept the part Ryan Cassidy had played in her life.

'He doesn't know.' Ryan's voice was cold and taut as he finished her sentence for her. 'He *doesn't know*,' he repeated in a very different way, his tone making Anna feel shiveringly cold as if slivers of ice had slipped slowly down her back. 'No wonder you're so uptight—you're afraid that Marcus Denton will find out the truth about your murky past.'

'Not at all!' Anna jumped in—far too quickly, she realised on a shiver of panic as she saw from the look of satisfaction on his face that her unthinking words had simply confirmed Ryan's suspicions, giving her away completely.

The smile that curved that wide mouth held a cold triumph that had Anna's hands clenching in the soft silk of her dress.

'And if he did find out——' Ryan ignored her outburst and continued in a coldly taunting voice '—what would happen then? Would that engagement——' once more those dark eyes flicked to her ringless hand, reminding her of the relationship she had implied earlier '—which obviously means so much to you still go ahead, I wonder? Or would Mr Denton think that a man of his social standing would need a wife whose background is similarly impeccable, not someone who——?'

'Stop it!' Anna broke in sharply, her voice high and tight in the quiet garden.

She couldn't bring herself to care that her reaction told him everything he needed to know, revealing how much his words had meant. Every trace of the sense of magic she had felt earlier had vanished, shattered into tiny fragments by the implied threat. The Regency rake, Mr Darcy, the man who had kissed her hand, they had all vanished, and in their place was a cold-eyed, cold-hearted man who had shattered her life in the past, and now could destroy her dreams of the future if he chose.

'If just to think of it worries you so much, then it seems to me that Mr Denton is totally wrong for you,' Cassidy went on, a frightening touch of triumph in his voice. 'Perhaps it's time he found out the truth.'

'So it's to be blackmail, is it?' Anna spoke dully, feeling drained and emotionally exhausted, with a dreary sense of inevitability. After all, this was what she had expected all along. 'What do you want from me? I don't have all that much money——'

'*Money's* not what I want from you,' Ryan responded curtly. 'I have more than enough of my own.'

'Then what?'

Anna felt as if an iron hand was squeezing her nerves, twisting them agonisingly. What more could he want from her? Surely not——

'I'll think of something—oh, don't panic, my lovely,' Ryan added sardonically, seeing the flare of fear in her eyes. 'It isn't your beautiful body I'm after. We went that way once before, remember? I don't think either of us would want to repeat the experience.'

Anna winced inwardly, clamping her teeth down hard on her lower lip to prevent a cry of pain escaping her. If she had needed any evidence of how little that night eight years before had meant to Ryan, then his callous declaration would have brought that home to her.

'You bastard!' she flung at him, driven beyond all self-control.

Ryan shrugged off the insult with a cynical smile.

'As you said, lady—I'm no gentleman.'

Abruptly he seemed to lose interest in baiting her, lifting his hand in an angry, dismissive gesture.

'Go back inside, back to your precious Mr Denton before he comes looking for you—you wouldn't want him to find us together, would you, Anna-Louise?'

Desperate to get away from him, Anna had moved even before he had finished speaking so that his last words were flung at her retreating back as she hurried towards the light and noise of the ballroom. She felt like Cinderella, coming back to reality on hearing the clock strike midnight, except that she was running *back* to the ball, not away from it, and it was no Prince Charming she had left behind but a man who had taken her innocence and her life and shattered both into tiny pieces for his own selfish pleasure, heedless of the fact that she was deep in mourning for the man she had loved—his own brother.

If she had feared that Marc would have missed her and become suspicious of her absence, requiring an explanation she was in no state to give him, Anna soon found that that was not at all the case. She didn't know how long she'd been away, whether hours or merely minutes had passed since she had gone out into the garden, but clearly Marc had been fully occupied all the time. He was still standing near the bar, wine glasses in hand, deep in conversation with a man whom Anna recognised as an established stockbroker.

At any other time she probably would have laughed, accepting the situation with resigned equanimity and a mental shrug. That was Marc; no one would ever change him. But tonight, with Ryan Cassidy's threats uppermost in her thoughts, hearing his voice inside her head saying, 'Surely if Mr Denton were concerned about you he'd have come looking for you,' she felt a sudden surge of anger and an irrational sense of betrayal at the way

that Marc had confirmed the lack of interest implied by
Ryan's comment so that she marched towards him, her
colour unusually high, sparks of annoyance in her green
eyes. The fact that Marc glanced up as she approached,
his only reaction being a casual nod of acknowledgement with no hint of apology added fuel to her anger.

'So here you are! I've been looking for you everywhere. You went to get the wine ages ago—I'm practically dying of thirst.'

'I was just coming.'

Marc's tone and the faint frown between his brows
told Anna that he was disconcerted by her outburst—
and not at all pleased. Knowing how ill-mannered he
considered public displays of emotion to be, she could
well imagine that he was embarrassed that she should
behave like this before his companion, and at any other
time she would have respected his opinions. But after
her encounter with Ryan Cassidy she felt as prickly as
a thorn bush and practically snatched at the glass he
held out, thinking privately that right now she could do
with something much stronger than champagne.

'Clive and I were just discussing those Eastman shares.'
Marc's very calmness was a reproof, an example of how
he expected her to behave, and Anna took a hasty
swallow of her drink, struggling to impose some sort of
control on her frayed nerves.

What *was* she doing? She needed Marc. Only tonight
she had finally admitted to herself how much it would
mean to her if Marc were to ask her to marry him—and
with Ryan Cassidy's threat hanging over her head she
couldn't afford to risk making any sort of false move
which might shatter those hopes once and for all.

'Then I'm sorry I interrupted,' she said quietly and
knew from Marc's brief smile that her apology had been
accepted and her world, which had been rocked danger-

ously for a moment, was once more back on its familiar foundations.

At the back of her mind, she heard Ryan Cassidy's voice saying, 'I'm afraid he's totally wrong for you,' and instinctively she lifted a nervous hand to her head as if to erase the worrying thought. She had always believed that Marc was her anchor, her stability, the final link with this world to which she so desperately wanted to belong, that without him she would be lost, adrift on a stormy sea in a rudderless boat, alone and vulnerable— a prey to men like Ryan Cassidy. But now she had to face the fact that that certainty could never be hers again. The foundations on which she had built her life had been eroded by Ryan Cassidy's reappearance in it. His presence in London was like a time-bomb, ticking away, and the terrifying thing was that she had no idea when it might blow up right in her face. Because of him, her relationship with Marc, which she had believed would provide the stability and security she sought, was now no longer the protection she had thought but had been transformed into a dangerous weapon in the hands of a callous and unscrupulous enemy.

She had no idea what Ryan might want from her; she only knew that she had no alternative but to wait until he let her know the price he demanded for his silence. And when he did, she vowed, if it were humanly possible, she would pay it, no matter what it cost. He had hurt her so terribly once; she couldn't let him destroy her life all over again.

CHAPTER THREE

ANNA knew that, once she had become aware of the fact that Ryan Cassidy was at the ball, however much she might want to she could not avoid him for the rest of the night. But with his threat of blackmail hanging over her she had hoped for a little more time in which to regain her composure, hide her disturbed feelings behind a mask of social ease, before she came face to face with him again.

As it was, she wished the evening was over; she felt emotionally drained and physically exhausted by the tension she felt, to which was added the strain of watching everything she said to Marc. But there were still a couple of hours to go, not to mention the drawing of the raffle.

'Ladies and gentlemen!' As if in answer to her thoughts, Gillie Ford's voice came over the public-address system, breaking into the hum of conversation in the supper-room. 'We are about to draw the raffle and announce the winners, so would everyone please make their way into the main ballroom? And have your tickets ready!'

The announcement had barely finished before Marc was on his feet.

'We'd better go and join Sonia and William——'

Grateful for the distraction from her disturbed and worrying thoughts, Anna was about to follow him when Gillie added something that made her freeze in her tracks.

'I'm delighted to be able to tell you that our guest of honour tonight—Ryan Cassidy—has graciously agreed to present the prizes.'

'Anna?' Marc's voice was impatient, annoyed at the way she was keeping him waiting, and Anna gave herself a reproving mental shake.

At least now she knew where he was. She was safe for the time being, she told herself, experiencing a wave of intense relief as she followed Marc out into the main ballroom and across to where Sonia and William were standing. If Gillie had persuaded Ryan to present all the prizes, that was likely to be a lengthy process, so surely she could relax for a while, knowing he was unlikely to bother her while he was occupied like this.

'Got your tickets?' Marc enquired, and Anna was disturbed by the way her stomach twisted rather queasily as she saw the gleam of an excitement that looked worryingly like avidity in his eyes.

Marc could afford to buy any of the prizes several times over, she reflected uncomfortably, and yet he was still excited by the thought of acquiring one of them for a tiny fraction of what it was worth. It was impossible not to contrast the array of luxuries on the table with the one raffle she had ever won in her days at college. Then the prize had been a bottle of supermarket plonk. But a moment later such thoughts fled from her mind as William nodded his head in the direction of a couple on the opposite side of the room.

'Have you seen who Gerald's with?' he asked, condescending laughter shading his voice. 'He's only brought the dreaded Tiffany with him.'

'Not Miss Coronation Street herself!'

Anna winced at the contempt in Marc's tone. She knew exactly who he meant. Tiffany Redburn was a very young, very beautiful and newly successful model, recently arrived in London from a council estate in Bolton. From the moment he had met her in the company of his friend Gerald, Marc had constantly derided her accent, her lack of sophistication, her often rather gauche behaviour.

'The very same—but it gets better. It seems she's wearing a very large and extremely tasteless ring.'

'Good God!' Marc's exclamation was one of disgust. 'The man must be losing his marbles.'

'I think she's rather sweet,' Anna put in hastily. The real truth was that Tiffany reminded her very much of herself when she had first left Yorkshire, before she had acquired the veneer of *savoir-faire* which had helped her present the right sort of image to Marc.

'Sweet enough to her own type perhaps.' Marc slanted a sneering glance in Tiffany's direction. 'And all right for a bit of fun for a while—but not to *marry*——'

'So there you are, Marcus! Where have you been hiding yourself?'

Gillie Ford's rather nasal voice broke in on them, and as Anna turned to acknowledge their hostess her heart seemed to stop beating, her blood turning to ice in her veins as she saw the tall, black-haired figure standing at Gillie's side.

She could have no hope that he hadn't caught Marc's damning remarks. The sardonic twist to his mouth, a cynically taunting lift to one dark eyebrow told her that he had heard every word and, to judge by the look of dark triumph in those blue eyes, he had already related them to her own situation, realising just how much stronger they made his own threats.

'I want you to meet Ryan—Ryan Cassidy—our guest of honour. We're so lucky to have him here, of course——' A coy, flirtatious glance was slanted at the man beside her. 'You can't imagine the trouble I had to persuade the wicked creature to come tonight.'

Anna had to struggle to suppress a grimace of distaste as she saw the smile which was Ryan's response to his hostess's teasing. Privately, she took the liberty of doubting that he had really needed any persuasion to come to the ball. After all, what man of his type would want to miss out on an occasion when, as guest of honour, he would be lionised and fêted, the centre of interest for every female present? It was much more likely that he had deliberately made a pretence of being reluctant in order to enhance his reputation for being difficult.

Marc's acknowledgement of Ryan was a casual inclination of his head.

'I'm glad Gillie persuaded you to come after all—you wouldn't want to miss out on one of the social events of the year.'

Anna didn't dare to try to interpret the look that crossed Ryan's face at Marc's comment, but he responded easily enough.

'Well, of course it's in a very good cause.'

'Oh, the youth centre...'

Marc's momentary pause gave him away, revealing the fact that he had forgotten Gillie's reasons for giving the ball, and, infuriatingly, Anna saw from the faint twist to Ryan's mouth that he had noted the slip, just as he equally obviously was aware of Marc's belated recollection of her own presence.

'This is my partner, Anna——'

'We've already met.'

It was said quite blandly, and no one but Anna could have read any darker meaning into it. But she had seen the tiny flick of a glance in her direction, the distinctly challenging gleam in his blue eyes in the moment that

Marc had described her as his partner and not the fiancée she had confidently asserted earlier, and knew that that apparently casual remark could easily catapult her into a dangerous minefield where one unwary step could mean something exploding right in her face. Her breath seemed to catch in her throat and she was sure Marc must hear the frantic pounding of her heart as he turned a questioning glance on her.

'I——'

'We met just now—in the garden,' Ryan put in after a pause calculated to last just long enough to have her stomach twisting in panic. 'We introduced ourselves then.'

So he wasn't going to say any more, Anna thought on a rush of relief that almost, but not quite washed away the tension that gripped her. But she had relaxed too soon.

'Your *partner* and I had an interesting talk...' This time there could be no doubt in Anna's mind that Ryan had meant to emphasise one particular word—and had meant her to know it, too.

'I—needed some air,' she blurted out awkwardly before Marc could ask her just what the 'interesting' conversation had been about. The questioning glance he turned on her dried her throat so that she couldn't have continued but, amazingly, it was Ryan who filled the uncomfortable pause.

'And I was looking for some peace and quiet.'

The feeling of being let off the hook was so intense that Anna actually sagged limply, leaning against the wall behind her for support. So he wasn't going to say any more—this time at least. For the first time she felt she knew exactly what was meant by playing cat and mouse. For how long would Ryan let this cruel game continue— and what would he demand as the price of his silence?

'Peace and quiet!' To Anna's relief, Gillie's voice broke into the undercurrents between herself and Ryan. 'Really, Ryan, you have to be joking! You'd only just arrived—and very late, too,' she added with a playful slap on his arm. 'You hadn't had time to get to the point of needing peace and quiet.'

'I'm not much of a party animal,' Ryan said flatly, no trace of his earlier affability softening the stark statement.

He had *meant* it, Anna realised with a sense of shock. This was no act, no careful living up to his reputation. And, remembering her own difficulties in learning how to cope with the large social gatherings which Marc and Sonia frequently attended, she found herself looking at Ryan Cassidy in a new light, searching his face for some sign that his smoothly charming manner was just a mask, hiding a very different person inside.

'In fact, it was just the idea of supporting your charity that made me come here in the first place.' The moment of honesty, if that was what it had been, had passed and Ryan was smiling again. 'And, of course, your eloquent persuasion—You're a very difficult lady to refuse. I never stood a chance against you.'

As he spoke he turned those stunning blue eyes on Gillie, looking deep into her face as if to convey the impression that, for him, she was the only woman in the room.

And he had had the effect he wanted, Anna reflected cynically, seeing the way Gillie blushed and murmured some inarticulate response to the blatant and outrageous flattery. She had been wrong, Ryan had not been being honest earlier; he had been playing with the other woman, manipulating her calculatedly.

How had he learned to flirt in this way? The Ryan Cassidy she had known had had no skills in that field at all. His attitude towards women had been more of the take-it-or-leave-it type—though that had apparently worked well too, to judge by the number of girls she had seen hanging on his arm. None of them had lasted very long, but it seemed there was always another to take the place of the last one he had discarded, apparently without a second thought.

'Well, now, I'd better go and put on my official organiser's hat.' Gillie's voice still held a shaken note, revealing the effect Ryan's behaviour had had on her. 'I can't wait to see who wins the major prize—it's very special indeed. Come along, Ryan, it's time you did your duty too.'

'So that's Gillie's famous back-street Picasso,' Marc commented as Gillie and Ryan made their way towards the stage. 'Not quite the roughneck we'd been led to believe—though I suppose the costume's deceptive. You'd have to see him in real life to know what he's actually like.'

Anna prayed that her thoughts didn't show in her face as she recalled just when Marc had seen Ryan Cassidy in real life, and precisely what his reaction had been. She could only be grateful that the dark shadows in the car park had hidden Ryan's face on that occasion so that even she would not have known who he was if he hadn't spoken.

In spite of herself she couldn't drag her eyes away from the tall, dark figure at Gillie's side. Ryan Cassidy looked even more devastatingly rakish in the brightly lit room than he had in the pale moonlight, and, recalling the threat he had made in the garden, Anna felt her legs weaken beneath her.

Even when the evening ended, would she be free of him? Was he simply enjoying his sick, tormenting game for this one evening, or did he really mean to take matters

further? When tonight was over would he let her go or
would he hunt her out, demanding the price he had decided on for his silence? How long would she have to
live with his dark, oppressive shadow hanging over her?

'And the first number is...'

Ryan had drawn the first ticket and handed it to Gillie
to announce the number. He looked very much at ease,
Anna reflected, totally unconcerned at being thrust into
the limelight like this—but then, all evening he had
shown little sign of being worried or ill at ease in such
sophisticated and affluent company, as Anna herself had
been when she had first become friends with Sonia and
Marc. Certainly, he had made no attempt to hide anything about his background in Empire Street as she had
done, she reflected ruefully, recalling the magazine article
Sonia had shown her. On the contrary, he had made sure
that people knew the exact truth—if only she had done
the same, then she wouldn't be in this worrying situation. But then Ryan had nothing to fear from people
knowing the truth. He obviously didn't care what people
thought of him—he never had.

Watching the smiling ease with which Ryan performed his role as prize-giver, a ready word on his lips
for every recipient, Anna couldn't help wondering how
one of 'those dreadful Cassidy boys', as her father had
always referred to the two younger brothers, had acquired such social grace, such *savoir-faire*, such *presence*.
Ryan Cassidy mixed perfectly with this sophisticated
London society, and yet there was an alien, untamed
streak in him, so that she had to admit that he also still
retained some essential part of the man she had known.
The old Ryan Cassidy was still there in the strong pride,
the 'take me as I am or to hell with it' self-confidence,
the refusal to compromise. And, just as in the past, the
present-day Ryan still had the power to frighten her,

make her want to run and hide, fearful of what he might do.

'Only one number out!' Sonia exclaimed in disgust, but Anna was totally unaware of what number had actually been called.

Watching Ryan, she couldn't help wondering what his father would think of the Regency costume, and a faint, involuntary shiver ran over her skin at the thought of Lawrence Cassidy Senior's probable fury if he could see the starched lace at his son's neck and wrist, the soft velvet of the jacket. Mr Cassidy had hated the thought of his sons being considered anything less than 'real men', which was why he had, if not tolerated, then at least turned a blind eye to Rory's wild activities but had exploded in a savage rage when he had discovered that Ryan, whose hopes of going to art college had been dismissed out of hand, had in fact been attending evening classes in the hopes of pursuing a career in a subject which his father considered was only for the weak and effeminate.

She had actually felt sympathy for Ryan then, Anna recalled. She had been just sixteen and she had called to see Mrs Cassidy, wanting to know exactly when Larry was due home on his next leave, and she had stumbled into a scene that had terrified and stunned her. Mr Cassidy had been purple-faced with fury, bellowing abuse at Ryan, who was white and drawn, his long mouth tight-lipped against all that he was holding back, and on the table between them lay the sketches, the paper, paints and brushes, bought, Anna knew from Larry, with the money earned from long hours of overtime in the local carpet factory, which his father simply saw as evidence of the fact that his son had disobeyed him.

Frozen in the doorway, she had watched in horror as the older man had gathered up every single item and flung them on to the open fire, smiling his satisfaction as the flames flared savagely, devouring them in a few blazing moments. Anna's eyes had gone to Ryan, fearfully expecting that he would launch himself at his father, that she would become involved in the sort of brawl that so often occurred outside in the street after closing-time on Friday or Saturday night. But Ryan had simply watched, stony-faced, until the last of the flames had died down and then, without a word, he had turned on his heel and walked out.

Impulsively, Anna had followed him, acting on an instinctive need to offer comfort, and she had caught up with him in the alley behind the house.

'Ryan——' Reaching out, she had caught hold of his arm. 'Ryan—wait!'

He had swung round, blue eyes blazing down into her face that was almost as white as his own.

'What the hell do you want?'

'I just wanted to say—oh, Ryan, I'm so sorry! I understand—I know just how you must feel——'

'You *understand*?' Ryan's laughter was harsh, savagely bitter. 'What would you know of anything I might feel? You don't even know I exist except as Larry's brother. You and your father don't think I'm fit to breathe the same air as you—and you say you understand me!'

'I was just offering sympathy——'

'Sympathy!' Ryan spat the word out as if it had a vile taste in his mouth. 'You can keep your bloody *sympathy*, Miss High and Mighty Miller—believe me, it's the last thing I want from you!'

He had wrenched his arm from her grip and stridden away, leaving Anna standing staring after him, the tattered remnants of her sympathy mixing with anger at his rejection of her, a lingering shadow of the fear she had felt earlier, and a strong feeling of disgust. Deep down, Ryan Cassidy was no better than his father. He was just an animal, a vicious, crude creature who could never understand the finer, gentler things of life.

It was then that she had decided that, whatever it took, one day she would get out of Empire Street; she would leave its dirt and ugliness to the Cassidys of this world, putting it far behind her—and with it the loneliness and isolation she had endured. And when that day came she would never look back.

A squeal of excitement brought Anna back to the present and she saw a young woman ecstatically waving her raffle ticket in the air as she hurried towards the stage. Anna watched expressionlessly as Ryan handed over the prize together with an enthusiastic kiss, which made her stomach lurch sickeningly.

Ryan had kissed her too—not just that gentle kiss on the hand this evening, in the garden, but years ago——

Anna's hands clenched into tight fists at her sides, her nails digging into her palms, as she struggled with the subconscious part of her mind which persisted in throwing up images of the hateful scenes she had thought long buried in the depths of her memory.

He had kissed her—caressed her, taken her, *used* her; there was no other word for the appalling way he had treated her.

On the night after the fight with his father, Ryan had left Forgeley, had disappeared out of her life—for good, Anna had believed. His parents had no idea where he had gone, but she suspected that Larry knew and kept his mother informed. Anna never asked about him, of course. After his harsh rejection of her offer of sympathy she had erased Ryan Cassidy from her thoughts altogether. Besides, her life was very full. She was growing up, working hard on the beauty therapy course; there was so much studying to do, the practical placements, the social life of the college, and—when he had leave—there was Larry. Larry who, as even her father was prepared to admit, was nothing like his loutish, tearaway younger brothers, who had always treated her with affectionate tolerance, as if she were a favoured child, but who now, surely, as she came to adulthood, must start to look at her in a very different light.

But then her father had died of a sudden massive heart attack, and she had been left alone in Empire Street, where she had to stay, at least until she finished her course. Without even her father's company, it had all seemed so much worse, so much more ugly and frightening, and Larry, the only person she could confide in, had been posted to Belfast and came home very rarely. In that dark time, the only thing that had kept her going was the fact that she was in her last year at college and the thought that in the summer, when she qualified, she would be given the key to her prison, the freedom from Empire Street and all it stood for. So she had worked harder than ever and had been rewarded by spectacularly high marks in her final exams.

Hot tears burned in Anna's eyes because to recall the day she had been given her final results also meant remembering the other appalling news which had arrived that day. Larry was dead, killed in an ambush near the Irish border—and it had been at his funeral that she had seen Ryan Cassidy again.

'*Anna!*'

Sonia's excited voice jolted Anna out of her unhappy reverie so suddenly that she stared at her friend with unfocused eyes, like someone emerging from a trance.

'Number forty-eight—you've won!' She snatched the tickets from Anna's limp hand and waved them in front of her face. 'Go and collect your prize.'

No! The refusal sprang to Anna's lips but died unspoken as she saw the way Marc was looking at her, the faint frown between his brows. He would hate it if, with everyone's eyes on her, she did as she wanted and dug her heels in, refusing to move. It would be just the sort of scene he could never tolerate.

With a struggle Anna pulled herself together. With those terrible memories now so close to the surface of her mind, her skin crawled at the thought of being even in the same room as Ryan Cassidy, let alone on the rostrum with him, but the presentation of the prize would take only a moment. She must hold on to that fact and try not to let her fear and disgust show in her face— though if he dared to try to kiss her she would very soon put him in his place, Marc or no Marc.

To her relief, it was Gillie who came forward to greet her as she mounted the rostrum, and in her hand was the envelope with the large red question mark on it. Numbly, Anna wondered how long she had been trapped in her memories of the past. She had thought that she had won some small item, but now she realised that the table behind Gillie was empty, and it was the final, major prize which she was to receive.

In spite of herself, her gaze went to where Ryan Cassidy stood, and as their eyes met she saw his mouth curve into a wide smile that, to the audience, must have seemed like one of warm congratulation. Anna, however, was close enough to see the light of triumph in those bright eyes, and the way they slid from her face and down, slowly and appreciatively, over the rest of her body. Suddenly the white dress, which before had appeared modest enough, now seemed to Anna to be almost non-existent, too revealing at its low neck, the delicate material almost transparent, and the gauzy shawl she wore offered no protection from that keen, assessing gaze. All the warmth of the overcrowded room seemed to leave her body as a shiver of apprehension feathered over her skin and an irrational feeling of dread twisted the nerves in the pit of her stomach. Praying that the audience would take the sudden rush of colour in her face as an indication of excitement at winning, Anna forced her attention back to Gillie.

'Congratulations!' Gillie enfolded her in a brief hug then pushed the envelope into Anna's suddenly nerveless hands. 'You lucky, lucky thing! Well, go on, open it!'

To her consternation, Anna found that that smile of Ryan's had actually affected her physically so that her hands were shaking as she opened the envelope and drew out the beautifully inscribed card it contained. In the moment that her gaze focused on it, two words seemed to leap from the paper and hit her in the face so that her mind reeled sickeningly.

It couldn't be true! Please let this be just a dream! Forcing herself to concentrate, she read the words printed on the card through from start to finish, and every trace of her earlier heightened colour fled from her face as she realised without hope of escape that this *was* true, it was no dream from which she could hope to wake. The urge to rip the printed card into tiny shreds was almost overwhelming, and as she struggled to resist it she became aware of the murmur of questions and comments which rose from the crowded ballroom.

'Well, what is it?' someone called out, but Anna couldn't find the strength to answer them. Now she knew the reason for that smile of triumph, and she felt as if she would never be able to form a rational thought again.

Dimly she became aware of Gillie stepping forward to stand at her side.

'Ladies and gentlemen, obviously Anna is too stunned with delight to be able to tell you what her prize is, so perhaps I'd better explain—and then I'm sure you'll understand her reaction. Our major prize tonight has come about through the generosity of one man—to whom we offer our deepest thanks. He has very kindly offered his time and talent to make this a very special prize indeed. Anna has won the opportunity to sit for her own portrait—painted by none other than Ryan Cassidy!'

'It would look better if you smiled,' a low voice, laced with cynical amusement, murmured in Anna's ear, making the small hairs on the back of her neck lift in apprehension. 'Your *partner* is obviously very pleased.'

With an effort Anna forced her eyes to focus and her hand clenched convulsively on the beautifully engraved card as she saw the broad grin on Marc's face, the way William was shaking his hand as if Marc and not Anna were the actual prize-winner. With a terrible sense of loss she recalled the almost greedy gleam in Marc's eyes before the start of the raffle, and knew with a painful sinking of her heart that, no matter how much she might wish to refuse this prize, Marc would never understand if she did. Fate had played right into Ryan Cassidy's hands; if he had fixed the draw himself in order to torment her even further he couldn't have arranged things better.

'I won't do it! I won't!' Unthinkingly, she whispered the words just loud enough for the man at her side to hear.

'I'm afraid you'll have to,' he returned just as softly, the silky menace in his voice shivering over Anna's sensitised nerves. 'Otherwise, what will your precious Mr

Denton think? You wouldn't want him to believe you
had some secret reason for turning down this opportunity, would you?'

There was no answer that Anna could give him; her
tongue was totally incapable of forming any words. She
was frighteningly and inescapably trapped, like some
terrified rabbit caught in a woodland snare.

CHAPTER FOUR

ANNA straightened her shoulders, adjusted, unnecessarily, the fit of her jade linen dress, drew a deep breath, and finally made herself ring the doorbell to Ryan Cassidy's flat, struggling against the impulse to turn and run as she heard its sound pealing through the hallway.

What *was* she doing here? How had she let herself be persuaded into going through with this? But then she had to face the fact that it had not been a matter of persuasion. Bitter honesty forced her to admit that she had never really had any choice in the matter.

Through the glass in the door before her she could now see a tall, dark figure descending the staircase, and her heart started up a rapid, uneven beat as she nerved herself for the coming meeting. At the ball she had tried to persuade herself that Ryan's interest in blackmailing her would last no longer than that evening, that she had only to put up with a few hours of his uncomfortable company, and that if she avoided making any mistakes that might make him angry enough to reveal who she was she would soon be able to get away to continue her life in peace. But now she found herself committed to who knew how many hours spent alone with him, and the prospect was not one she anticipated with any degree of pleasure.

'You came, then?'

Absorbed in thought, Anna hadn't been aware of the door opening, but suddenly Ryan stood before her, tall and lithe, and somehow even more disturbing in the loose white T-shirt and worn denim jeans that clung to every muscular inch of his long, powerful legs. Gone was the Regency rake of the ball, and in his place was a forcefully masculine creature who could never be thought of as part of a dream but was visibly, potently flesh-and-blood reality. *This* Ryan, she was sure, would never go on his way quietly and leave her alone. The dreamlike time in the garden had long since been pushed from her mind as the fantasy it was; what she was faced with now seemed like a nightmare from which she couldn't waken.

'Did you think I wouldn't?' Unease made Anna's voice high and tart.

A wryly ironic smile twisted the long mouth, and Ryan's blue eyes gleamed with a devilish sort of amusement.

'Well, let's just say that when I imagined the reaction of whoever won first prize in the raffle the thought of their looking as if some terrible ghost from the past had suddenly returned to haunt them wasn't exactly what I had in mind.'

'Well, what else did you expect?'

That mention of a ghost from her past had come too close to the truth for comfort, forcing Anna to subdue a wave of panic before she could continue.

'I suppose you thought that any woman would be thrilled at the chance of spending some time alone with "the sexy hunk of the art world",' she snapped, quoting the magazine article which Sonia had shown her then immediately wishing she hadn't as it gave away the fact that she had taken the trouble to read it—something a man with an ego like Ryan Cassidy's was likely to interpret as being an indication of an interest that she was far from feeling.

'On the contrary, I thought that anyone—man or woman—would be at least a little pleased to think they would have a chance to procure a "Ryan Cassidy masterpiece".'

The mocking inflexion he gave the words told Anna that he was quoting too, that he had read what had been written about him in the article—and hadn't been too impressed by their hyperbole.

'At no cost. I'm sure your friend Mr Denton would have been delighted at the chance for such a potentially lucrative investment,' he finished.

Which was exactly the argument Marc had used to persuade her to come here today, Anna reflected privately, unexpectedly irritated at the way Ryan had unerringly put his finger on something which had bothered her at the time. She hadn't dared to declare outright that she didn't want Ryan Cassidy to paint her, brilliant though his work was—and even Anna, prejudiced as she was, had to admit that he had a wonderful talent—because she had been afraid that to do so would arouse Marc's suspicions, but she had made it plain that she wasn't exactly keen on the idea. Marc had been stunned and disbelieving, and had set himself to persuading her to change her mind—and, of course, being Marc, the main arguments he had used had been based on the financial aspect of the matter.

'You've no right to say such things—you don't know Marc at all!'

How Anna wished that Marc *had* used other reasoning, that he had talked of the artistic merits of Ryan's work or had expressed a wish to have a portrait that captured her own beauty, so that she could have flung such arguments in Ryan's sardonically smiling face, denying his implication of materialism angrily.

'True,' Ryan agreed. 'But that was never a consideration that stopped you in the past, was it?'

Not at all sure what he meant, and far too irritated to try to work it out, Anna was torn between a fear of antagonising him too much and a strong desire to turn on her heel and march away, but at that moment Ryan stood back and held the door open wide.

'Are you coming in, then?'

'I thought you'd never ask.' Anna winced at the sound of her own voice; it was childishly petulant and sullen. She had to get a grip on herself quickly; angering Ryan would be a very dangerous thing.

'I'm afraid we're right at the top.' Ryan led the way, bounding up the stairs two at a time so that Anna, in her high-heeled sandals, had to struggle to keep up with him. 'That's one of the reasons why I chose this place—for the light.'

He reached the top landing a good two minutes before Anna, and her mood was in no way improved by the fact that he wasn't even breathing rapidly after the four flights of stairs while she felt decidedly puffed and embarrassingly pink-cheeked as she caught him up.

'Here we are——' Ryan flung open a door. 'Come in and make yourself at home.'

As soon as she stepped into the room, Anna saw exactly what he meant by saying that he had chosen the flat for the light. This room must originally have been one of the attics, and had been carefully and skilfully improved and extended. Being so high up, there was no one near by to overlook them, and the whole of one wall had been replaced by huge windows so that the overall impression was one of air and space. It was almost like being up among the clouds in a glass-sided plane.

'Oh, this is wonderful!'

Slowly she turned full circle, taking in the whole of her surroundings, and realising as she did so that the effect of the light came not just from the enormous windows but was enhanced by the décor and furnishings as well.

The room had clearly originally been two smaller ones, made this size by knocking down a dividing wall. The walls were painted a soft cream, which kept the overall effect of brightness, but with its rich colour gave an impression of warmth, not the stark coldness of pure white. There was no carpet, the floorboards had been sanded and varnished to a clear, glowing pine, with a huge green and cream rug forming an island beside the fireplace, surrounded by three squashily comfortable-looking settees in the same rich green. To Anna's surprise, there was only one painting in evidence, a huge rural landscape, its bold green and gold patchwork of fields and trees picking up and intensifying the more delicate colours of the room.

'What a glorious place! You were lucky to find this.'

Anna couldn't erase the note of envy from her voice, put there by the memory of the tiny, scruffy bed-sitter which had been all she could afford when she had first started work. How had Ryan Cassidy of Empire Street come to live in a place like this? When she had imagined his flat, she had never expected anything so elegant, so sophisticatedly simple, so utterly delightful.

'How did you manage to get hold of it? Did you sublet it from someone working abroad or something?'

'It isn't sublet—or rented from anyone—it's mine.'

Ryan's voice was curt and the way that wide, expressive mouth had tightened told Anna that he had seen through her question, going straight to the thoughts behind it—and the trouble was that she couldn't deny them. Without being aware of it she bit her lip in consternation at her mistake.

'What's wrong, Miss Miller?' Ryan questioned sardonically. 'Not quite what you expected from one of "those damn Cassidys", is that it?'

'I——' Anna couldn't find any way to answer him because now that she stopped to think she was thoroughly disconcerted to find that she felt rather ashamed of her attitude.

Why *had* she been so surprised to find Ryan in such surroundings? After all, he was an artist—and an exceptionally talented one, honesty forced her to admit. Hadn't everything she had ever heard about him indicated that, by utilising the forceful combination of that wonderful talent with an equally powerful one for sheer hard work, he had indeed, as Sonia had said, pulled himself up by his own bootstraps, leaving Empire Street as far behind him as she had done—in some ways at least?

'It's just that——' She hunted for a way of explaining herself, knowing that the cold anger conveyed by the dark irony of his tone was fully justified. Thinking of Empire Street, and his parents' scruffy terraced house, she had been guilty of prejudice. 'I didn't expect you to have actually bought somewhere to live in London. After all, as you said, your home is in the north, and you gave the impression of never wanting to leave there.'

As soon as she said the word 'home' a pang of distress shot through Anna, bringing with it a vivid picture of the Cassidy house. Scruffy it might have been, but, at least when Larry and Mrs Cassidy had been there, it had always seemed like a home, while her house was just a place where she and her father were forced to live, where Edward Miller had never decorated or improved anything because, he said, it wasn't worth it—he wasn't staying there any longer than he had to.

'True,' Ryan conceded more quietly. She seemed to have appeased him for the moment at least—the cold light dying from his eyes and the tension that pulled his face muscles taut, drawing the skin tight across his high cheekbones, easing perceptibly, softening his expression. 'And I'd prefer to be in Yorkshire if I could, but sometimes I need to be in London—to work here— so I thought it would be better to have a base here, where I could set up a permanent studio.'

One strong hand gestured towards a door at the far end of the room, which, presumably, opened on to that studio, and, recalling belatedly exactly why she was here, Anna took an automatic step towards it.

'Not yet.' Ryan's quiet voice stilled her. 'I prefer to talk to my subjects first—get to know a bit about them— and see their faces in all sorts of different expressions, moods, lights, before I actually start work. So why don't I make some coffee and we'll just talk——?'

'I don't have all that much time,' Anna put in hastily. That comment about getting to know her had set her nerves jangling. She had come here reluctantly in order to have her portrait painted; she hadn't reckoned on having a heart to heart with Ryan Cassidy as well.

'How long does a cup of coffee take?' The ironic note was back in his voice, the sound of it seeming to scrape over Anna's sensitive nerves like rough sandpaper. He knew exactly how she felt, those observant artist's eyes missing nothing of the play of feeling across her face. 'It's all ready, so if you'll just sit down and make yourself comfortable...'

He was heading for the open door to the kitchen as he spoke, and, left with no alternative but to do as he suggested, Anna made her way towards one of the settees.

It was only when she was actually about to sit down that she realised that the settee was already occupied. A large ginger and white cat uncurled itself from among the cushions, greeting her with a small miaow and an interested sniff of its pink nose. Reaching out, Anna began to stroke the cat from head to tail, feeling some of her tension ease as she did so.

'You're honoured,' Ryan commented when he returned with a tray of coffee to find the cat snugly ensconced on Anna's lap, purring ecstatically. 'Redford doesn't usually take to strangers.'

'Redford?' Anna echoed, intrigued. 'Is that his name?'

Ryan nodded, a wry smile curling his lips. 'Maeve called him that. I found him abandoned in a ditch near my home in Yorkshire—he was only very tiny then—and when she first saw him he still had blue eyes, which, with the reddish-gold fur, made her think of Robert Redford; and of course he's red-furred...'

He grimaced apologetically at the pun, the expression turning into a wide grin of amusement at her exaggerated groan.

Anna was highly disconcerted to find that the appeal of that boyish grin struck home to her heart, knocking her mentally off balance so that she almost asked the questions which were on the tip of her tongue. Who's Maeve? she wanted to know; was she someone he knew in London or Yorkshire? And just what sort of relationship did Ryan have with her? It was a rather special, intimate one, to judge by the warmth in his voice when he spoke her name. But realising just in time that to ask such a thing would reveal far too personal an interest in Ryan, she hurriedly changed her question into an innocuous comment instead.

'Well, your cat doesn't seem to mind me—in fact, I think he was glad of the company.'

'He's probably feeling rather lonely,' Ryan agreed. 'I haven't been at home all that much this week, and, like me, he's probably missing Yorkshire. He's a real wan dering tom-cat—he needs his garden to roam in, not to be cooped up in a flat like this.'

Very much like his master, in fact, Anna thought privately, acknowledging once more that wild streak, the untameable quality she had sensed in Ryan. On the surface he might appear the sleek, cultured sophisticate, but she knew the real man behind that urbane mask, and *he* was very different. When she found her mind wandering on to the possibility that Ryan and his pet might share other characteristics, notably the casual sexual appetite for which tom-cats were notorious, she hastily dragged it back on to less disturbing subjects.

'So why did you bring him with you? Surely he would be happier at home if there was someone to look after him.'

Someone like Maeve, perhaps, a small, uncontrolled part of her mind suggested, bringing with it a totally unexpected prick of discomfort that made Anna shift uneasily in her seat, causing Redford to dig in his claws protestingly.

'I tried that, but it didn't work out. The daft creature pined—wouldn't eat—so I had to go and collect him and bring him here. Milk? Sugar?'

'Oh, just milk, thanks.' It took Anna a couple of seconds to respond to Ryan's question, her thoughts being centred on the—to her—incongruous thought that this tough, forceful male should have such a soft spot in his heart for the bundle of ginger and white fur on her knee that he would leave his work and drive a round trip of several hundred miles simply because his pet was unhappy. The unexpected revelation made her feel strangely warm inside, a warmth that was mixed with a disturbingly uncomfortable feeling, one that was disconcertingly close to envy of Redford. Marc would never do any such thing, even for her.

'So, tell me about yourself. Marcus Denton introduced you as his partner.'

Ryan had settled himself on the settee opposite and was now lounging back in his seat, obviously ready to begin that 'getting to know her' process which she so dreaded. But at least if they talked about her work she was reasonably safe. That way she could keep things impersonal, avoid the quicksand of the past and the events which had so devastated her life. But she didn't know for how long she could just talk when her skin felt as if every inch was afflicted by a particularly painful form of pins and needles and she wanted to demand to know just what it was he wanted from her, what form his blackmail would take.

'That's right—well, perhaps it would be more accurate to say he was my backer. You see, I——'

Glancing up suddenly, Anna froze as she realised that Ryan had picked up a pad of paper and a pencil and was sketching her face with swift, confident strokes.

'Do you have to do that now?' she asked sharply.

'Don't let it worry you,' Ryan returned easily, not pausing in what he was doing. 'It's just a few casual sketches—nothing permanent. Just try and forget about it.'

Forget about it! There was no way she could do that when every couple of seconds she was subjected to a swift, keenly searching glance from those vivid blue eyes before he turned his attention back to his drawing, the soft scrape of the pencil on the paper seeming unnaturally loud to Anna's suddenly over-sensitised hearing.

'Relax.' Ryan's voice was soft, cajoling. 'Talk to me. You were saying that Denton's your backer—in what way? What sort of business?'

'Natural cosmetics and skin care. It's something I became interested in a long time ago, and for some years

I'd been making products for myself. It all started in a very small way—some of the clients in the salon I managed tried some of my creams and they were very popular...'

Unconsciously, Anna found that she actually was relaxing, the nervous tension seeping out of her as enthusiasm for her subject took over. Those quick, probing glances were still directed at her every few seconds, but, surprisingly, she now found that they didn't disconcert her because Ryan somehow managed to communicate interest and encouragement at the same time as he was observing her closely.

'Eventually it got to the point where I couldn't supply as much as people wanted, working on my own, so I took on a couple of workers while I stayed on at the salon in order to make sure I had enough money coming in until the business was large enough to support all of us. That was where I met Sonia, and, through her, Marc. Is there something wrong?'

Ryan's busy pencil had suddenly stilled, and he was looking down at his sketch pad, frowning slightly. At her question his sapphire-blue eyes lifted, narrowed assessingly and strangely darkened by some emotion Anna could not interpret, then abruptly Ryan shook his head both in answer to her question and as if to rid himself of whatever strange mood had suddenly gripped him.

'No—I'm sorry——' Ripping the page from his pad, he tossed it aside with an impatient gesture. 'Go on— I'm listening.'

Anna found it difficult to recover her train of thought. Her own mention of Marc's name, and Ryan's behaviour, had set her on edge once more. Was Ryan's apparent interest in her life simply that of getting to know his sitter as he had claimed, or was he looking for some-

thing more—something connected with her and Marc—
that he could use against her?

And there was something else, something equally un-
nerving. From having come to a point where, if she
hadn't actually forgotten that he was sketching her as
she spoke, at least she had come to accept it, now she
was intensely aware of it once more, but in a new and
infinitely more disturbing way.

She had never realised what a sensual experience it
was to have someone draw her, to know that Ryan's attention was concentrated totally on her, visually at least,
those flashing blue glances seeming to have the force of
a shaft of lightning, the whisper of the pencil on the
page making her nerves tingle as if it were actually
stroking against her skin. She was suddenly totally aware
of her own body, the sun warm against her back, the
brush of her hair against her face and shoulders if she
moved her head, the feel of her clothes on her skin. And
that awareness was heightened by her sensitivity to the
physical presence of the man opposite her, his long body
indolently relaxed apart from those swift glances in her
direction, that constantly moving hand.

'So you met Sonia . . .' Ryan prompted.

'Yes, she was a client of mine and she'd bought some
of my original creams and loved them. She introduced
me to her brother and we became friends——' Belatedly,
Anna remembered her precipitate declaration on the
night of the ball that Marc was her fiancé, and hastily
added, 'And we've been inseparable ever since.'

Surprisingly, Ryan did not make the sardonic comment
she had expected, but seemed totally absorbed in his
sketching.

'Marc encouraged me to try and make a go of my own
business. He gave me a loan to set up in the first little
shop; I paid it back in the first year after we'd opened.'

Anna didn't try to conceal the pride that rang in her voice, and she felt a glow of delight when she saw the admiration in the look Ryan turned on her.

'Since then, things have gone from strength to strength. Marc's put more money into the business and I've provided the know-how. Just a few weeks ago we decided to become legal partners. We have ten shops now, three in London, and the others scattered around the south——'

Something had changed, Anna realised with a jarring sense of shock, her voice failing her suddenly. Outwardly, everything seemed the same, Ryan still sprawled on the settee, his pencil still moving over the paper, but there had been a new and distinctly worrying quality to the look he had given her, and, now that she looked at him more closely, she saw that that frown was back between his dark brows, making her stomach clench in apprehension as his attention became fixed on the paper before him, her tension growing as she saw the movement of his pencil gradually slow, become suddenly completely still.

'I—we—hope to have more branches soon,' she stumbled on, trying to fill the uncomfortable silence that had descended. 'Marc thinks that——'

Ryan's sudden violent curse broke into her awkward words, making her freeze in shock, and Anna felt as if an icy hand had reached out and gripped her heart as some sixth sense alerted her to what had happened.

The fragile truce which had existed since she had first arrived was over. Ryan Cassidy, the artist who claimed he simply wanted to get to know her, was gone, and in his place was the man who had hurt her so badly—the man who had the power to destroy her present by telling Marc about her past. And now she was sure that at last he was going to tell her the price of his silence.

CHAPTER FIVE

'WHEN I said that I wanted to talk to you——' Ryan's voice was harsh '—I wanted to get to know *you*, Anna-Louise, not some Marc Denton clone!'

It was ironic, Anna thought through the whirl of panic that filled her head, that in all the years she had lived in Empire Street Ryan Cassidy had been the only one who had ever used the correct version of her name, the one her father called her by. Everyone else had considered it far too fanciful and had quickly abbreviated it to plain Annie, not bothering to try to get their tongues round the proper form of Anna. But Ryan had always said Anna-Louise, usually in the sort of aggressive, hostile tone which, as now, made her hate the sound of the words.

'My name is *Anna*.'

'Oh, yes, it's Anna to your partner, and your fine London friends—but you were always Anna-Louise to me, weren't you, my lovely?'

'Don't call me that!' Heedless of Redford's cry of protest, Anna got to her feet in a rush, depositing the cat on the floor. 'I'm not your——' her tongue wouldn't form the word, feeling strangely thick and clumsy in her mouth '—your anything!' she managed clumsily and flinched inside as she heard his cynical laughter once more.

'You haven't changed a bit, have you? You may be better dressed, have a new hairstyle, you might mix with your high-society friends—you've even tried to lose your accent—but you're still the same Lady Anna-Louise.'

'And just what do you mean by that?'

That comment about losing her accent had stung. It seemed painfully ironic that now, all these years later, Ryan should say that she had tried to lose it when in fact, in the days when she had lived in Empire Street, she had tried so much harder to speak in the way her father believed was correct, trying for his approval, but actually only earning his criticism as he detected traces of the northern way of speech in her voice.

'You and your father always thought you were too good for the rest of us, didn't you, my lovely? And you still do.' Uncannily it was as if Ryan had picked up on part of her thoughts. 'Now I see why you weren't so keen to come here. I suppose you thought you would be slumming if you mixed with the likes of the Cassidys of Empire Street. So why are you here now, I wonder? Did Marcus Denton feel that the potential investment value of your portrait was too good to turn down, even outweighing the taint of your mixing with the sort of louts you were forced to grow up with?'

'Don't be ridiculous! You don't think I'd——'

The swift lifting of Ryan's dark brows, the sudden flash of realisation in those stunning eyes made Anna curse her runaway tongue.

'You haven't told him? That could be a foolish mistake.'

'Only in that it has forced me to come here today...'

Ryan couldn't genuinely believe that she might have told Marc everything since the night of the ball. He must know that there was no way she would be here with him now if it weren't for the threat of exposure that he held over her. And if he believed that Marc knew the truth, then surely he would have cancelled the sitting, said he couldn't paint her portrait. After all, to a man of his type, there would be no pleasure in going along with this except for the cruel enjoyment of watching her suffer under his threat to betray her secret. And yet he had almost seemed to imply that he had been giving her a second chance—waiting to see if she had nerved herself to tell Marc everything.

But no, that didn't fit with everything she knew about Ryan Cassidy's character. The hard, uncaring man she knew him to be would never give anyone a second chance.

Only now did Anna become aware of the fact that, although she had been standing for some time, Ryan had never moved from his place on the settee, where he still lounged, apparently totally at ease. Which was strange, because in the past few minutes Anna had felt as if he had dominated the room so much that she was stunned to realise that he wasn't even standing, let alone towering over her threateningly.

She wanted to get out of here—as quickly as possible—but that need warred with the knowledge that if she left Ryan would simply interpret her behaviour as running away; it would make him aware of just how much she feared him and the things he could reveal to Marc—and that would give him too much of a hold over her. So she stayed where she was, frozen into immobility by her indecision, until Ryan spoke suddenly, making her start nervously.

'Sit down, Anna-Louise.' His voice was quiet but held a note of command that had her moving automatically to her seat before reason reasserted itself and she stopped dead.

'I think I'd better be going.' Anna hated the way her voice shook, revealing too much of her inner disquiet for comfort.

'*Sit down*!' Ryan repeated more emphatically, his tone making it plain that it would be dangerous to disobey so that Anna hastily slumped down on the settee without a thought for elegance or dignity. 'You and I need to talk.'

'We have nothing to talk about.' Anna forced the words past lips that seemed to be made of wood, they were so stiff. 'I know exactly what you're going to do.'

'Oh, do you?' One black eyebrow lifted in sardonic enquiry. 'So you can read my mind, can you?'

'Mind-reading has nothing to do with it! It's quite obvious that Marc knows nothing about my past life in Empire Street—and that it could damage me badly in his eyes if it were all to come out.' She might as well admit it, she told herself; it was obvious that Ryan would not believe her if she tried to deny it. 'And you've always hated me, so now you'll take a great delight in holding that fact over me.'

'I always hated you?' Ryan put a strangely questioning intonation on the words. 'You don't know the half of it, my lovely. One thing's for sure, though—you and I have one hell of a lot of unfinished business between us.'

'No, we don't!' Anna made a move to get to her feet, get away from him, but a warning flash from those blue eyes had her sinking back into her seat again, her legs suddenly feeling too weak to support her.

'There's nothing—*nothing* between us!'

To her consternation and incredulous fury, Ryan picked up his pencil again and started work on another sketch.

'But there was once,' he murmured silkily.

'And you plan to tell Marc all about it!' Anna's voice was high and uneven with fear.

'Not necessarily...'

Anna's precarious grip on her self-control snapped completely. Ever since the night of the ball, Ryan had been playing with her cruelly, in the way a cat played with a mouse. He had kept her dangling, knowing she was frightened by his threats, but never letting her know just what it was he wanted from her, and she'd had enough.

'Just what is it you're after? What exactly do you want from me?'

The seconds before he answered seemed to drag out interminably, stretching Anna's nerves so tight that she felt they might actually snap under the strain. Then, very slowly, Ryan lifted his head and smiled with deceptive sweetness.

'I want to paint your portrait.'

'You——' Anna couldn't believe she had heard him right. 'You—*why*?'

Ryan's broad shoulders lifted in a nonchalant shrug.

'That's my business. Let's just say you intrigue me, and you have the sort of face I want to try to capture on canvas, and that's when I do my best work—when I see someone I really *want* to paint.'

Anna knew she was gaping like a stranded fish, her mouth opening but no sound coming out. This couldn't be happening! Hearing the barely controlled antagonism in Ryan's voice a few moments earlier, she had been convinced that he had had enough of playing around with her, that now he was going to discard the affable, sociable mask he had shown her since she had arrived, and let her know just what she was going to have to do—or how she was going to have to pay the price for his silence. The first thing she had expected was that he would declare that it was time they dropped the pretence that she was here to have her portrait painted, and so she couldn't believe that Ryan actually wanted to do just that. But that couldn't be *all* he wanted, could it?

'How can you paint me when you don't even like me?' she said hesitantly.

'Like?' Once more that offhand, dismissive shrug lifted Ryan's shoulders. 'Like doesn't come into it—I'm not looking for an affair, or even friendship, so your character isn't important. I just want to paint faces— and I like your face very much.'

Anna hated the way that colour washed her cheeks, as she fought against the illogical, irrational sense of pleasure those last words had brought her. They hadn't even been intended as a compliment, except as a back-handed one. 'I like your *face*,' he had said, leaving a great deal out.

'And I know you——'

'No, you don't! You knew me once—a long time ago. A lot can change in eight years.'

'But some things stay just the same. You may think you've come a long way from the Anna-Louise of eight years ago, but inside you're still just the same person.'

Anna shivered involuntarily as a sensation like the trickle of icy water slid down her back. In one way at least she was still the same person as she had been eight years before. She still found Ryan Cassidy the most disturbing and frightening man she had ever met.

'But you don't want to paint my thoughts!'

'No...' Those bright blue eyes were on her face once more, strangely dark, and holding her troubled green gaze with a power that was almost mesmeric. 'But I want to paint the effect those thoughts have had on your face.'

Ryan's tone was soft, almost a caress, and Anna suddenly recalled how she had felt a short time earlier, when he had been sketching her, the sensual awareness that had flooded her body. Rationally, she might try to deny it—she desperately wanted to deny ever having felt any such thing—but, in spite of her fear and anger, in spite of the fact that she hated this man, she knew that those undercurrents were still there, tugging at her like some powerful magnetic force, so that her longing to leave, to get away from his disturbing presence warred with a crazy desire to stay so that she felt that her mind might actually tear apart under the strain.

She didn't like the sensation one little bit. It made her feel as if the intervening years had been stripped away and she was once more the naïve eighteen-year-old she had been, so lost and lonely that she would turn to any man for comfort—even Ryan Cassidy. She had to get a grip on herself. There must be some way she could get the conversation off this dangerous track and back on to safer, more conventional topics. But with Ryan were there any safe topics?

'And would that be enough to overcome the way you feel about me?'

One black eyebrow drifted upwards as if querying some part of her question.

'I told you—you intrigue me, and I have to be interested in someone—there has to be some spark, some attraction before I can really paint them.'

At last Anna saw a possible diversion and seized on it gratefully.

'And what if someone who didn't interest you or——' The word seemed to stick in her throat as an echo of the disturbingly sensual tone he had used earlier sounded inside her head. 'Or attract you—had won the raffle prize; what would you have done then?'

'Ah.' To her surprise, Ryan considered the question seriously. She had thought that he would ignore it, refusing to let himself be distracted when he clearly knew just what she was trying to do. 'That's a tricky one.'

His gaze slid away from her face to the pencil and sketch pad now lying discarded in his lap, then moved to his hands, almost as if he were asking them her question, trying to find out if they would use their talent successfully even if his mind and motivation wasn't fully behind them.

'I suppose I'd have had to go through with it. After all, I'd promised Gillie my work as a prize for a cause I support whole-heartedly, so I'd have to produce something—but——' he lifted his hands in an expressive gesture '—I'd do as good a job as I could, and I'm sure the winner would have been very pleased with it—but I wouldn't. It wouldn't be my best work. There would be something missing.'

'Is that why you wouldn't paint Pamela Curtiss?'

In spite of herself, Anna was intrigued by the things Ryan had said, and she was deeply curious about the way he would answer this question. No one had ever managed to get Ryan to give a satisfactory explanation of his refusal to paint the industrialist's wife.

'Didn't she interest you?' she prompted.

How could any man not be interested in Pamela Curtiss? Surely any red-blooded male would be drawn to the former model's long mahogany-coloured hair, her perfect oval face, deep brown eyes and glorious figure.

'Pamela Curtiss is an empty-headed bimbo.' Ryan's tone was scathing. 'And neither she nor her husband would be able to tell good work from bad—but it wasn't her I objected to.'

'Then what?'

'Damn it, Anna!' Ryan's sudden explosion rocked Anna back in her seat. 'You lived in Forgeley—you knew those factories Drew Curtiss owned! They were just sweat-shops—slave labour. My father worked in one of those places until he died, and I did too for a while—worked every hour God sent for a pittance of a wage. Men like my father worked themselves into the ground

to earn Curtiss the fortune he now has. I couldn't have
painted his wife; I'd have kept thinking about my mother
and the way she had to struggle to make ends meet. When
I looked into that beautiful, empty face I'd have seen
the lines on my parents' faces—the strain, the exhaustion,
and everything I felt would have shown through in my
work. He could never have paid me enough to overcome
that.'

'And with me?'

The question slipped out before Anna had time to
consider whether she really wanted him to answer it.
Ryan's mention of Forgeley and his parents had rocked
her, reminding her of their shared past so that she
couldn't think straight. So his father was dead—but what
had happened between him and Ryan in the intervening
years? It was hard not to feel a pang of envy for the sort
of family feeling Ryan had expressed so forcefully; she
had never really known anything like that.

And if she was honest she hadn't expected such strong
principles from Ryan Cassidy. She would have thought
that he was much more likely to hold out for every penny
Curtiss would offer him, dash off some indifferent work,
then take the money and run.

'With you?'

Those amazing blue eyes swung up to her face, the
force of their appraising gaze so strong that Anna actually shrank back in her seat. Then suddenly Ryan's
expression changed, an ironic smile curling one corner
of his wide, mobile mouth.

'What is this, Miss Miller? Could you be angling for
compliments?'

'No!' The denial was too sharp, too swift, and Anna
hastily tried to soften its effect. 'I was just wondering
whether—seeing as I was the one who won the prize and
you're morally obliged to paint me as you promised Gillie

you would—whether you'd just do the job or—if you could—really paint me.'

It was clumsily, awkwardly put, but she saw the subtle change in Ryan's expression and knew that he had understood exactly what she had been trying to say.

'You can rest assured that I will have no trouble with your portrait,' he said with a strange mixture of curtness and unexpectedly warm sensuality that made Anna's toes curl inside her soft leather sandals, setting her nerves tingling as they had when he had been sketching her. 'Oh, yes,' he went on almost to himself, 'I could definitely paint you.'

Which came as near as damn it to admitting that he was attracted to her, Anna realised, stunned to find that her mouth and throat were suddenly painfully dry and her heart was beating in an uncomfortably jerky rhythm.

She couldn't be attracted to this man! She had always felt nothing but disgust and hatred for him, she told herself frantically. But then from the hidden recesses of her mind came memories of one night when those feelings had been overcome, memories of his kisses, his caresses——

No! She hadn't been thinking straight then. She had been lost, in despair, and Ryan had taken advantage of her, callously adding to her sense of devastation over the loss of Larry.

It had to be because of Larry that she felt this way, she rationalised desperately. Ryan might not physically resemble him strongly, but they *were* brothers, and some echo of the sound of his voice, some gesture, some movement must have reminded her of the Cassidy she had loved with all the innocence and devotion of which her young heart was capable. She had to be seeing Larry in his brother—she couldn't feel anything for *Ryan*.

'I'm glad about that,' she said stiffly, remembered pain making her voice distant and cold. 'You see——'
Suddenly she knew how to hit back, show her contempt for Ryan Cassidy once and for all. 'I really would like my portrait painted because I plan to give it to my——'

A flickering, challenging sidelong glance from those blue eyes made her bite back the word fiancé, which she would have preferred to use.

'To Marc for his birthday.'

Ryan hadn't liked that; she could tell it from the way his head went back, his eyes narrowing swiftly, and she felt a rush of relief at having destroyed those uncomfortably sensual undercurrents that had tugged at her.

'Marcus Denton?'

The name was a sharp question touched with dark aggression, which deprived Anna of the ability to speak and forced her simply to nod silent agreement. Ryan seemed about to add some further—and probably, to judge from his expression, angry—comment, but then he evidently had second thoughts and remained silent, though his opinion was clearly expressed by the way his mouth was clamped into a thin, hard line.

'You don't approve?' Anna found that her voice would function again though it wasn't quite strong enough to express the satire she aimed for.

'Approve?' Ryan echoed the word ironically. 'What's to approve or disapprove? When I've finished this portrait it will be your property—that was the arrangement. You can do what you like with it—give it to Denton, hang it in the coal shed or chop it up for firewood—it's no business of mine.'

The dismissive tone Ryan used stung sharply, making a nonsense of Anna's earlier belief that he had come close to admitting that he found her attractive. Or was he simply angry that she should consider giving away his precious painting? Did he actually believe that she would want to keep the portrait as a memento of the time she had spent with him while he was working on it? Remembering the other women who had fawned over him at the ball, she could well imagine he might be under that illusion. Well, she'd take pleasure in pulling that particular rug from under his feet!

'Oh, I could never do that!'

She had pitched her voice at exactly the right level, the hint of shocked consternation just enough to have his head lifting in an uncontrollable movement of surprise. Knowing that, for once, she had caught him off guard, Anna pressed home her advantage, leaning towards Ryan to emphasise the importance of what she was about to say, and letting her green eyes open wide, looking straight into his blue ones in an expression of candid sincerity.

'That would be a criminal waste, Mr Cassidy. I'm not such a fool that I don't know that to own a genuine Ryan Cassidy original is better than having money in the bank. After all, Marc——' she emphasised the name carefully '—tells me that I couldn't possibly have a better investment.'

A golden flame of anger flared in those eyes, which were now so dark that they were almost black, and Ryan's skin appeared to be drawn tight over the hard bones of his face, etching white lines of fury around his nose and mouth.

'That's just the sort of mercenary comment I'd expect from someone like Denton,' he snarled, lurching suddenly to his feet, swinging away from her to snatch up her jacket. 'Well, I think we've said everything there is to say——'

Although in the few seconds he had had his back to her he had obviously made an effort to rein in his temper, get himself back in control, anger still smouldered under the smoothness of his words, like the embers of a fire that a breath of wind could soon fan into a raging inferno once more.

'So perhaps we'd better call it a day. When would it suit you to come again so that I can really get down to work?'

Never, Anna was tempted to retort. She didn't want this painting, and she certainly didn't want to pose for it. She would never even have considered doing any such thing if she hadn't won that damned raffle. Even though one part of her longed to see what this exceptionally talented artist would make of her portrait, and in spite of the fact that it wasn't going to cost her a penny, she didn't believe that the end result, wonderful though it might well be, would be worth having to endure Ryan Cassidy's abrasive personality for however long it took to complete it.

'I don't think——' she began unevenly, and saw his dark brows lift in an expression of cynical amusement.

'Chickening out?' he questioned satirically. 'Running away again?'

The softly emphasised 'again' stung bitterly, and Anna felt anger boiling up inside her like lava in a volcano, threatening to spill out in a furious, destructive flood.

'I'm not running away!' she exploded. 'It's just that I don't think I'll take up the offer of the raffle prize after all. I only bought those tickets for a bit of fun and to help Gillie's charity. I don't want this portrait, and I think——'

'And how are you going to explain to dear Mr Denton when you can't give him his promised birthday present?'

Silky irony laced Ryan's enquiry so that for all their softly spoken gentleness his words still had the bite of acid.

'Oh, Anna-Louise, lass, what reasons are you going to give your—partner—to justify turning down the chance of such a wonderful investment?'

Anna-Louise. Ryan hadn't reminded her of the hold he had over her—he hadn't needed to; his use of her real name had done that for him. Hidden behind the deceptive gentleness was the deliberate warning that if she 'chickened out' then he would have no compunction about making sure that Marc discovered some pretty unsavoury facts about her past.

'The raffle prize isn't negotiable, Miss Miller. It's the portrait or nothing...'

'You mean it?'

The *painting* really was to be the price of his silence. Anna couldn't believe that that was all that Ryan wanted. Where was the catch in all this? Because, with Ryan Cassidy, there had to be some catch.

'I mean it.' Ryan's tone was coldly emphatic. 'The portrait or——' There was no need for him to finish the sentence.

Determined to hide the fact that his words had hit home, Anna struggled to school her face into an expression of carefully controlled indifference, one that she hoped successfully hid the fact that, deep inside, she was close to panic at the thought of the possible consequences if she didn't agree to what he wanted. When she spoke she was amazed to find that her voice was as steady as she would like, though the ruthless effort needed to keep her emotions in check made it sound hatefully cold and brittle.

'Perhaps you're right, Mr Cassidy. I really shouldn't turn down such an opportunity. Let me see...'

She reached into her handbag and pulled out her diary, making a great pretence of studying it as a ploy to gain a little time to calm her racing heart and get her erratic breathing back under control.

'I'm afraid I'm busy all next week,' she lied, ignoring two completely free afternoons. 'Sunday afternoon is the only time I have available—but perhaps you prefer not to work at weekends?'

It was impossible to iron out the tiny lift to her voice which betrayed her hope that if Ryan said no, he wouldn't work on a Sunday, she could claim to be booked up during the week for the next month or so, and then perhaps this whole project could be dropped quietly without justifying his accusation of running away, and so, hopefully, escaping the blackmail threat he had implied. But Ryan had no hesitation in pulling that particular rug from under her feet.

'Not at all,' he replied smoothly. 'I don't give a damn when I work. In fact, when I'm painting, day or night doesn't matter to me. I'm quite capable of forgetting about time completely. And, unlike you, I can work whenever the opportunity arises. I'm not tied to dates and times in a Filofax.'

The bite of satire in his voice told Anna that Ryan strongly suspected that at least some of the appointments she had claimed for the coming week were fictitious—which, of course, they were, she admitted privately, holding her diary half closed in the irrational fear that those keen, clear eyes might actually see through its leather cover and detect the empty spaces on its pages.

'So, shall we say next Sunday—would one o'clock suit you?'

Knowing she had been outmanoeuvred by an expert, perfectly checkmated, Anna had no alternative but to nod agreement.

'I'll be here,' she said flatly.

'You'll be here.' Ryan's soft-toned agreement sent cold shivers down Anna's spine. 'If you're wise you'll be here. Because I tell you this, my lovely; I want to paint your portrait, and I have no intention of going back up north until I do. So if you don't come on Sunday I'll come looking for you—and I'll find you. Now that I've caught up with you at last, the whole of London won't be big enough to hide in if you try to run away from me again.'

CHAPTER SIX

'Now that I've caught up with you at last, the whole of London won't be big enough for you to hide in if you try to run away from me again.'

Ryan Cassidy's words haunted Anna as she struggled through the next week, trying desperately to absorb herself in her work, fill every waking moment so that she didn't have time to think. During the day at least she almost succeeded, but there were other times, particularly in the darkness of the night, times when there were no business decisions to be made, no letters to dictate, no telephones to answer, nothing to come between her and the memories that now would no longer be held back.

She hadn't always lived in Empire Street. The first seven years of her life had been spent in very different circumstances, in a comfort and elegance that bordered on luxury—the only sort of life her father had ever known. A southerner himself, he had been born and brought up in Kent, the only child of wealthy parents, his father owning a large country estate. Edward Miller had always known that he would inherit the land from his parents and so had never learned any skill or taken any job.

However, when his father died and he came into his inheritance at the age of thirty-five, it was to discover that the estate was much more run-down than anyone had ever believed. Paying death duties drained even more of its resources and from then on the slide into ruin was swift. Anna's father had had to declare himself bankrupt and sell the family home to meet his debts. Knowing that the cost of living was much cheaper in the north, he had taken his wife and young daughter to Yorkshire, where he had been forced to take on unskilled—and therefore low-paid jobs just to keep a roof over their heads.

When Anna's mother had died five years later, Edward seemed to have lost heart, the final straw being when he was made redundant only six months afterwards. Then he had been forced to face the fact that they could not even afford to continue to live in the modest semi which they rented. That was when they had moved to Empire Street. If Anna had hated that place and the change in their lifestyle, her father had never recovered from the move.

And now, if she closed her eyes, she could see Empire Street in her mind, the ugly, smoke-grimed terraced houses with their rotting window-panes and peeling paint on the doors. She could hear again the roar of motor-bikes, the taunts of the gangs of youths, the slurred singing of drunken Saturday night home-goers—singing that so often degenerated into fist-fights which had to be broken up by the police. In the week following her first visit to Ryan's flat it seemed as if she had lived through her entire life in Forgeley over again until, inevitably, the flood of memory had culminated in recalling the final appalling cataclysm on the day of Larry's funeral.

Even after eight years, bitter tears pressed against the back of Anna's eyes as she remembered how she had felt on hearing that Larry was dead. For over five years, ever since she had begun to take an interest in the opposite sex, Larry Cassidy, with his tall, muscular body, burnished copper hair and glowing green eyes had been like a god to her, the object of her total devotion, and the one bright, beautiful thing in the ugly, sordid world in which she was forced to live.

Larry had had a wide, infectious smile and a ready laugh, and, unlike the other boys, who plagued her mercilessly, shouting abuse or suggestive comments at her in the street, he had always been kind to her. He had never taunted her about the way she spoke or her name or her father's refusal to let her mix with the other occupants of the street. True, he had sometimes called her 'Duchess', but his teasing had been gentle and he tolerated the difference between them much more than anyone else. That was probably because he was so much older than her. He had been twenty-one when she had first seen him, a fully-grown man, unlike his brothers, who, with just a year between their ages, were teenagers like herself.

And, of course, soon after she had moved to Empire Street, Larry had joined the army and had learned a very different way of life from that of the back streets of Forgeley. He was at home all too rarely, never often enough or long enough for Anna, but when he was there things seemed so much brighter, so much better.

As she had grown to maturity and her body developed into womanhood, Anna had needed those moments of happiness all the more as the comments and suggestions, the behaviour of the youths who lounged on the street corner became more crudely sexual and threatening. One night, when she was fifteen, she had been cornered by a gang of four of them, who had demanded that she kiss them, becoming angry and dangerously aggressive when she refused. Terrified and distraught, she had been on the point of screaming when Larry had appeared and, taking in the situation at a glance, had come to her rescue. He had had to return to his regiment the following day and Anna had been terrified that, without his restraining presence, something similar, or worse, would happen again, but to her astonishment she was left completely alone—two of the boys even seeking her out to apologise—and she knew that, even though he wasn't there, she had Larry to thank for her reprieve.

So when Larry had been killed, barely a year after her father's death, Anna had been devastated. She had moved through her days like a pale, wan ghost, unable to feel any pride in her achievements in her exams, unable to think, even to cry. She attended Larry's funeral in a grey haze of pain, unaware of anyone around her, until, at the graveside, the sound of running footsteps had broken into her enclosed world and, glancing up, she had looked straight into the drawn face of Larry's youngest brother.

Ryan Cassidy had looked even worse than she felt. His skin was grey under the tan he had acquired somewhere in his two-and-a-half year absence, and those vivid sapphire-blue eyes were dull and lustreless, dark shadows lying like heavy bruises underneath them. His hair was long, reaching well over the collar of his shabby jacket, and tangled by the wind, giving him a disreputable, gypsyish appearance. He had halted on the edge of the crowd as if unsure of his welcome back into the family which he had abandoned so long ago.

And so he should be, Anna thought, jolted out of her mourning by a flash of anger. She knew how much his mother had suffered from not knowing where he was, how she had worried herself sick over what might be happening to him. But then her eyes met Ryan's pain-filled gaze and the anger was washed away on a wave of sympathy far stronger than the one he had repulsed so savagely on the night he had left Empire Street. After all, he had loved Larry too, loved him and lost him, and that at least was something they could share. Intuitively understanding his need to get closer, be as near to his brother as he could be for this last time, she moved aside, opening a path for him to where his mother and father stood.

Ryan Cassidy's blue eyes flashed Anna a brief but intense look of gratitude, and as he moved past her she heard him murmur, 'Thanks, sweetheart.'

That was the last straw, those two brief words, spoken in a voice that was so like his brother's—that dearly loved voice that she would never hear again. Blinded by the tears that had refused to flow until now, she turned and ran, stumbling, away.

Hours later, when the storm of grief had abated, she found that she couldn't bear to stay in the house any longer and, pulling on a lightweight jacket over the black skirt and blouse she had worn all day, she went out, walking blindly, not caring where she went until, inevitably, she ended up at the cemetery. She didn't know how long she stood there, staring down at the grave with its covering of flowers, but she hadn't heard anyone approach and so she jumped like a startled cat when a quiet voice behind her said, 'I know just how you feel.'

Spinning round in shock, Anna threw herself off balance, and would have fallen if Ryan Cassidy's hands hadn't come out to grip her arms, holding her steady. In the gathering dusk his face seemed colourless, his eyes just dark, impenetrable pools.

'Larry——'

It was the only word she could get out, the word that had repeated over and over in her head in an endless litany of pain since she had first heard the news.

Ryan made no response, but his grasp on her arms tightened, and, as if drawing some of his strength from that contact, Anna found she could speak again.

'Why did it have to happen? *Why*?'

She saw his dark eyes go to the grave and then swing back to her face.

'I don't know.' Ryan's voice was sombre, low and husky. 'If I could answer that, I wouldn't be here myself.'

'How—how long have you been here?' How long had he been standing there, silently watching her?

'A while. You looked as if you didn't want to be disturbed, and I wasn't exactly in the mood for conversation myself. I couldn't stay in the house. They're holding a real Irish wake in there—I needed some time on my own.'

His hands moved on her arms, sliding up to her shoulders in a way that was almost a caress, and as he came closer Anna could smell the scent of whisky on his breath. Suddenly her sense of self-preservation came to life again. This was Ryan Cassidy, who in the past had mixed with the rough louts who had made her life such a misery, and who had been living God knew where or how for the past couple of years. He had filled out a lot since she had last seen him, grown broader, stronger, no longer a youth but a fully grown man—and she was alone with him in this dark, deserted place, and he had been drinking. Involuntarily she shivered apprehensively.

'You're cold!' To her surprise Ryan sounded genuinely concerned. 'Come on, I'll take you home—I've got my car here.'

Numbly, Anna let him lead her away from the grave, but when they came out on to the road and he would have steered her towards the car she stiffened and tried to pull away.

'No—I'll walk.'

'It's nearly four miles and you look fit to drop already. Don't be stupid, Anna-Louise—get in the car.'

He pushed her towards the open door as he spoke, and, not daring to risk the possible consequences of resisting, Anna let herself be manoeuvred into the seat. The short journey back to Empire Street was completed in total silence, but when they were actually at her front door Ryan reached out and took the key from her hand, inserting it in the lock himself.

'I'm coming in with you,' he declared firmly. 'You shouldn't be alone at a time like this.'

'No!'

A whirl of conflicting emotions warred inside Anna's head. She didn't want him in her home; she had always been afraid of him, perhaps never more so than now— and yet she couldn't bear to be on her own any more, she would welcome any company, even Ryan Cassidy's.

'I don't want——'

'Please——' Ryan's voice had changed suddenly and Anna was stunned to catch a note of almost desperate appeal in it. 'I need to be with someone too.'

Something in his dark, shadowed face, the unhappiness in his voice, tugged at her heart, already raw and vulnerable after the stress of the day, and in spite of herself Anna found that she was weakening.

'I'll make some coffee.'

She needed something to do, something to keep her mind off the dark, brooding figure of Ryan Cassidy sitting there in her tiny front room—for the first time ever, she realised with astonishment. Her father had never let any of the Cassidy boys cross his threshold. So why had she done so? Because he was Larry's brother. Because, in spite of the differences in his and Larry's colouring, Ryan's height and build reminded Anna of his brother, and if she closed her eyes his softly accented voice could be taken for that older, much-loved voice that she would never hear again. By letting Ryan Cassidy stay, she was keeping Larry with her for just that little bit longer.

'Where have you been all this time?'

Anna's question came jerkily, asked just for the sake of saying something when the coffee had been made and she and Ryan were sitting opposite each other, the silence that had descended as soon as they had entered the house threatening to become oppressive.

'Spain.' Ryan's mouth twisted wryly as he glanced down at his hands, their bronzed skin dark against the white of the mug he held. 'That, as everyone's been saying, explains the tan.'

'You found work there?'

The dark head nodded agreement. 'A labouring job. The pay's almost non-existent, but I've learned how to live very cheaply.'

'But what about your painting?'

For the first time a tiny hint of a smile touched Ryan's lips.

'Labouring sees me through the days—at night I've been working in hotel bars, turning out pastel portraits for the tourists to take home as souvenirs.' His sudden laughter was harsh, bitterly sardonic. 'I'm a one-man conveyer-belt, churning them out by the dozen, but it's good practice—and it pays a lot better than farming.'

'And what does your father think about that?' Anna's voice rose nervously on the question, fearful of a violent response.

'He's accepted it.' It was said apparently casually, almost thrown away with a nonchalance that didn't quite hide the darkness underneath. 'He's lost one son—he doesn't want to lose another.'

'Larry.' Anna's face clouded as Ryan's words touched on the shared sorrow that had brought them together. Her hands clenched into tight fists in her lap as she struggled with the tears that threatened once more. 'Oh, God, I miss him so much!'

'Do you think I don't know that?' Ryan's voice was harsh with an inexplicable hostility. Then, as the tears Anna fought against welled up and slid down her cheeks, his tone changed abruptly. 'Oh, for God's sake, girl, come here and let me hold you!'

Beyond caring whether it was wise or safe, unable to think of anything except the need to be held and comforted by someone—anyone—Anna left her seat in a hurried, blundering movement, kneeling on the carpet beside him and flinging herself into his arms.

'I know, my lovely.' Ryan's soft words barely penetrated the storm of anguish in her head. 'I know, I know...'

His arms were as tight as a vice around her, crushing her up against the hard wall of his chest, and she clung to his warmth and strength, strangely grateful for the painful power of his grip that seemed to counterbalance the agony inside her. For the first time in days she felt as if there was still something left in the world, something firm and dependable, someone she could share her loss with. She could hear Ryan's heart beating strongly under her cheek, the scent of his body was all around her, and instinctively she curled her own arms about his narrow waist, holding him almost as tightly as he held her.

Immediately something changed. Ryan's grip on her loosened, becoming more gentle, and one hand slid up to cradle her cheek as he turned her face towards his, his eyes suddenly very dark, with only the tiniest hint of that vivid blue at their outer edge.

'Anna-Louise.' It was a husky whisper, barely audible, and sounding as if it had been forced from a painfully dry throat. 'Dear God, Anna-Louise——'

The next moment he was kissing her, his lips snatching greedily at her face as if in desperation, and after a second's stunned shock Anna found that she was responding, kissing him back with equal fervour, needing this contact, this closeness. Their mouths crushed together, bruising, demanding, as if by the sheer force of their kisses they could obliterate the horror of the day that had brought them together. Anna's hands were in Ryan's hair, twisting in the midnight-dark strands, holding him closer, because he could never be close enough.

Just when Ryan's hands moved to her body, she could never have said, only becoming aware of their urgent caresses as a heightening of her own need, intensifying the frenzy of longing that seemed to be burning her up the way a forest fire raged through drought-parched woodland, destroying the emptiness inside her. Hands that were clumsy with desperation tugged at the buttons on his shirt, her only thought that she needed to touch him, feel the living warmth of his skin against her own. Only then would she feel free of the burden of despair she had carried with her for days. She was so intent on what she was doing that she barely heeded the fact that her own blouse and skirt had been wrenched away, the fabric ripping in Ryan's rough haste.

She felt Ryan's hands on her breasts and hips, his lips trailing a path of fire over her body, and cried aloud at the whirlwind of sensation that assailed her, the spiralling crescendo of desire that was so sharp, it was almost a pain. She wanted him as she had never wanted anything in her whole life, needed to know, through him, that life could still go on, that she could still feel, and she knew a sense of perfect rightness when Ryan's voice, thick and rough, echoed her own thoughts.

'I want you, Anna-Louise—God but I want you! I want this——'

'Yes,' Anna broke in on him almost angrily, adrift on a sea of yearning, knowing that only one thing could assuage the hunger in her. 'Yes! Yes! Yes!'

As he moved over her, her hands clenched on his shoulders, her fingers digging into the hard muscles of his back as if she could actually physically force him to become one with her.

'Anna-Louise!' It was a choking sound, seeming strangely desperate to her ears.

'Now—now!' Fear that even now he would withdraw from her made her voice strong and resolute, and she heard his cry of surrender as he abandoned himself to his own need.

The raw, burning pain that ripped through her made Anna freeze in horror, her body rigid, rejecting this invasion, and in that moment the full realisation of what she had done came home to her, her mind reeling sickeningly as she faced the truth.

She had turned to Ryan in despair, in the bitter anguish of her loneliness, and that despair had made her too weak, too vulnerable. It wasn't *Ryan* she wanted, it was *Larry*—but Larry was dead, lost to her forever. She could never give him her love, and the sense of loss and pain had combined with Ryan's superficial resemblance to his brother to seduce her into a moment of appalling madness that all the wishing in the world could never undo. And Ryan had taken full advantage of the situation. He had taken the love that should have been Larry's.

Oh, Larry! Larry! Weak tears slipped out of the corners of Anna's eyes, sliding down into the tawny hair spread out on the carpet around her. If she had felt lost and bereft before, it was as nothing when compared with what she was experiencing now. Even the pain in her body had receded to a dull blur. The real, the savage agony was in her heart.

She didn't know how long the horror of her thoughts held her frozen, only becoming aware of the fact that Ryan had moved when a draught of cold air shivered over her body. Forcing herself to focus on the present again, she realised that he had flung himself away from her, getting to his feet and snatching up his clothes, pulling them on with rough, jerky movements.

'Ryan?'

Anna felt she had to speak, though she would have much preferred to remain silent. Her voice sounded hoarse and rusty as if it had not been used for a very long time.

He swung round violently, his shirt still in his hands. His eyes glittered with a feverish fury, looking unnaturally brilliant above the pallor of his cheeks, and she could see how his tanned chest rose and fell with every ragged and uneven breath he took.

'Isn't this the point at which I'm supposed to ask if it was as good for you as it was for me?' he snarled viciously, the force of his outburst making Anna curl into a tight, defensive ball as if his words had been actual physical blows rained on her vulnerable flesh. 'Perhaps in our case I'd better change that to—was it as bad for you——?'

He broke off the sentence with a savage shake of his head which was far more expressive than if he had continued, 'as it was for me.'

'I——' Anna began, meaning to say, 'I don't understand,'—and she didn't. He had got what he'd wanted, hadn't he? So why was he so terribly, so blackly furious? But Ryan didn't let her finish.

'Don't say a word, Anna-Louise. It would be better if you didn't—I couldn't be answerable for the consequences otherwise.'

He was pulling on his shirt as he spoke, his haste, every movement speaking eloquently of his desire to be gone—as quickly as possible.

'Where are you going?' Even though he had told her not to speak, Anna couldn't hold back that question.

'To——' He bit off whatever he had been about to say, substituting with succinct cruelty, 'I'm going home.'

Home? Now? He couldn't mean it! Even Ryan Cassidy couldn't be so callous as to leave her now, like this. But why not? a small inner voice questioned. She knew what such men were like; her father had warned her often enough. Men who wanted only one thing, and when they'd got what they wanted couldn't be seen for dust. Suddenly a strong sense of pride came to her rescue.

'I'd like my clothes,' she declared in a cold, stiff little voice.

He flung them at her as if simply to touch anything that belonged to her would contaminate him, and she gathered them close, not yet having the strength to put them on but simply using them as a blanket to cover her nakedness from those terrible, blazing blue eyes.

'And I'd like you to get out at once.'

'Don't worry,' was the unflatteringly swift response. 'I have no desire to stay here a moment longer.'

Ryan stamped his feet into his boots and looked around for the jacket which he had slung over the back of a chair on his arrival. Snatching it up, he flung it over one shoulder, not bothering to put it on.

'I wish I could say it's been nice knowing you, Anna-Louise,' he threw at her from the doorway. 'But I was brought up always to tell the truth. But I'll say one

thing—I'm not Larry, and never will be; you picked on
the wrong Cassidy, lady——'

'I'm not Larry, and never will be.' The words seemed
to hang in the air as the door slammed behind him, and
in a fury of rage Anna grabbed every cushion within
reach and flung them after him, the thud as they hit the
wall a totally inadequate expression of the hatred boiling
up inside her.

'You picked on the wrong Cassidy, lady——' She
didn't need anyone to tell her that. It was impossible to
believe that Ryan could even be part of the same species
as gentle, kind Larry, let alone his brother. Ryan wasn't
a man, he was an animal, a callous, selfish, cruel animal!

Practicality forced her to dress though her hands shook
so badly that she could barely fasten the buttons on her
blouse. The cuff on one sleeve was almost ripped off
and as she stared at the evidence of Ryan's brutality the
protective bubble of anger burst and she collapsed back
on to the floor, abandoning herself to her dejection.

Ryan Cassidy had been in her house for barely an hour,
and in that brief time he had managed to devastate her
life completely. She had thought that their shared loss
had brought them together; instead it seemed that Ryan
had had no thought of anyone but himself and his own
selfish lust.

Only now, far, far too late, did she recall how, often
in the past, when she had called at the Cassidys' house
to see Larry, she had looked up to find Ryan watching
her, his eyes as dark as they had been tonight. And there
had been all those times when his friends, members of
the gang that he and Rory mixed with, had called after
her that 'Ryan Cassidy fancies you.'

A sour taste filled Anna's mouth and a wave of nausea
gripped her as she forced herself to review the events of
the evening from the moment Ryan had come up behind

her in the cemetery. He had said that he had been
watching her for some time—perhaps even then he had
been thinking not of his brother as she had believed, but
of the fact that he had always wanted her, and forming
a cold-hearted plan to seduce her by offering a pretence
of sympathy.

And she had fallen for it! Furiously, Anna cursed her
foolish naïveté. She should have known what he was like!
At the beginning she had suspected some such thing, but
Ryan's skilfully assumed act of unhappiness, his calculated appeal to her own loneliness had driven all
thought of self-preservation from her mind. She had believed that he was feeling as desolate as she was, and,
for the second time, had offered him sympathy, only to
have it snatched from her and flung back in her face.

But this time he had taken something else as well—
he had taken her innocence, her love for Larry, her life,
and shattered them all into tiny pieces.

There was only one thing she could do; a sudden sense
of resolve pierced the fog of misery that clouded Anna's
mind. She could not face the thought of ever seeing Ryan
Cassidy again, couldn't bear to continue to live in Empire
Street with the prospect of him coming home to visit his
parents always there to haunt her. With her father and
Larry gone, her course finished, there was nothing to
hold her here any more. The house was no problem. The
rent was paid until the end of the month, and the
landlord was welcome to the shabby furniture in lieu of
notice.

Wearily Anna dragged herself to her feet and made
her way upstairs to pack a case. An hour later, when the
taxi she had ordered arrived, she told the driver to take
her to the railway station. She would take the first train
that came in, she decided. She didn't care where she went

as long as it was far away from Ryan Cassidy and from Empire Street, which she was now leaving for good.

And if she had needed any reinforcement of how little that night had meant to Ryan, Anna thought despondently as she lay sleepless in the darkness of her bedroom, then meeting him again would have driven it home to her at once. She had lived with the scars left by that particular episode for eight years of her life but to Ryan all it meant was the opportunity for some cold-blooded blackmail.

Ryan had used her callously, without a care for her feelings, eight years before, and now he was doing so again, and she had to find some way of living with the fear of what he could tell Marc if he chose. If Marc found out the truth about her past, would he still want to marry her? In spite of the warmth of the night, Anna shivered, admitting with painful honesty that she could have little hope that Marc would ever forgive the way she had lied to him. And if he ended their personal relationship, then what would happen to their business connections? Surely Marc would want to dissolve that partnership as well. She would lose every one of her hopes and dreams for the future in one blow. Anna shuddered at the thought of such a prospect.

She *had* to make sure that Ryan never told Marc the truth. He had said that as long as she co-operated with him by posing for her portrait then he would do nothing—but when the painting was finished, what then?

CHAPTER SEVEN

'THIS is an amazing room! It's like an Aladdin's cave, with treasures everywhere!'

Having anticipated her sitting for the portrait with something close to dread, Anna had returned to Ryan's flat on Sunday afternoon in a state of tension, not expecting to enjoy a single moment of the session, and in fact the first few minutes of stiffly awkward politeness were exactly as she had thought they would be. But then Ryan suggested that they move into his studio, and from the moment she had set foot in the other room Anna had been entranced by the large, airy room, flooded with light from the same sort of huge windows as those in the living-room, and the collections of brushes in all sorts of shapes and sizes, paints in every colour imaginable, all the clutter of Ryan's work, so that she had been unable to hold back a cry of delight.

'I never really realised before just how similar our jobs are,' she went on, studying the array of brushes before her. 'I'm not an artist like you, of course, but the tools of our trade are very similar.'

'Don't put yourself down,' Ryan surprised her by saying. 'I'd be willing to bet that some of your clients would prefer your skills to mine. After all, you use them to enhance their looks—I merely reproduce their features.'

'Now who's putting himself down?' Anna exclaimed. 'You can't describe your ability as "merely" anything— you're brilliant, and you know it!' A sudden thought struck her, making her think back over what Ryan had just said. 'Do you never flatter in your paintings?'

Vivid blue eyes met hers in a look of direct and open honesty.

'I paint what I see; flattery isn't the truth,' Ryan said quietly and something about his voice, and the way his gaze held hers, made Anna feel suddenly shiveringly cold and then burning hot.

So how would he paint her? She couldn't help wondering what sort of truth he would reveal in the portrait. And, even more disturbing, would he paint Anna Miller or the Anna-Louise he had known all those years ago? Because the truth was that she didn't know how Ryan Cassidy saw her at all.

'I remember how hard I had to save in order to buy my first set of kit before I started my beauty therapy course,' she said hastily, blurting out the first thing that came into her head in order to fill the taut silence which had descended, and to distract herself from such uncomfortable thoughts. 'I treasured every item in it as a result.'

She would have preferred to leave it there, but honesty forced her to go on.

'It was only then that I realised how dreadful you must have felt when your father destroyed your paints and brushes that day.' Her voice faltered, weakened by a sudden rush of nervousness as she wondered how he would react to her touching on the past in this way—and that scene in particular. 'I thought I understood something of what you felt, but, looking back, I realised that it didn't even come close.'

Just for a second, looking into his darkened eyes, she saw the flash of some violent emotion in them and tensed instinctively, fearing a repeat of the hostility he had turned on her that night. But a moment later heavy lids hooded Ryan's eyes, hiding their expression from her, and his broad shoulders lifted in an offhand shrug.

'It was all a long time ago.'

To him, perhaps, Anna thought, but, standing here now, with Ryan, dark and distant, beside her, the paints and brushes on the table before them, she felt almost as if she had gone back in time and was reliving the scene over again—only this time she saw it with the understanding of hindsight, saw just how devastated he must have been, and how inadequate her words of sympathy must have sounded.

To cover her unease, she launched into a string of questions, wanting to know what everything was for, how it was used, and Ryan answered her questions easily, showing no impatience to get down to work.

'I never imagined you as a businesswoman,' he said eventually, a gleam of something close to amusement in his eyes as he watched her sort through the tubes of oil paints, exclaiming her delight at the amazing range of colours.

'When you talked to Larry about what you wanted to do, it was the creative side of things you were most involved in. You could talk about make-up and colour for hours.'

Anna swung away towards the windows, ostensibly to get a better light on the colour of the tube of paint she held, but really so that the fall of her tawny hair concealed her expression as her mind flinched away from the memory of those times in the Cassidys' tiny front room when she had poured out to Larry the excitement and enthusiasm she felt about the beauty therapy course for which she had applied. Not wanting to share Larry with anyone, greedy for the little time she had with him, she had been openly resentful of the dark, intrusive, and, to her, threatening figure of his younger brother, and had openly ignored any contribution he had made to the conversation until Ryan had stormed out, slamming the door behind him.

'I really thought that you'd specialise in that area—that one day you'd end up doing make-up for films or television.'

'I thought so too.' The catch in Anna's voice was a reaction to the way Ryan had intuitively picked up on the way she had been thinking at the time. 'But later, when I actually started the course, I found it was the more basic things that interested me—make-up's just the surface glamour. And then when I found an old book of recipes for skin and hair care in a junk shop I decided to try some of them for myself. It started out as a hobby, but I found it so absorbing that it pretty soon became more than that.'

Suddenly becoming aware of the way he was studying her, those amazing eyes noting every movement, every gesture, every fleeting change of expression on her face, Anna felt a rush of embarrassed colour flood her cheeks.

'I'm sorry—I'm keeping you from working——'

'Take your time——' Ryan's gesture dismissed the fact that such a short time earlier he had declared that he didn't want to waste time, so they'd better start work at once. 'I don't just work with my brush, you know. As I said, I prefer to get to know my subject first.'

He hadn't taken the time to get to know her eight years ago, Anna thought on a rush of bitterness that shattered her relaxed mood.

'No, I think we'd better get started—I don't want to be here all day.'

He hadn't liked that last remark—she knew it from the flash in his eyes, and suddenly it was once more as if she had slipped back into the past, as if she were seeing the nineteen-year-old Ryan who had opened the door to

her when she had called round on the first day of one
of Larry's periods of leave.

'He's not here,' he had said abruptly, not needing to
ask what she wanted. 'He and Mam have gone into town
and won't be back for at least an hour.' To Anna's
amazement he had actually stepped back, opening the
door wider. 'But you can come in and wait if you want.'

Anna could just imagine what her father would think
of that. Larry, he could tolerate. In his opinion, the eldest
Cassidy son had at least tried to better himself—he had
a good position in the army, was steady, responsible and
polite—but Ryan was a different matter entirely. He
might not be as much of a hell-raiser as Rory, but his
reputation as a womaniser was second to none, and with
her father's warnings sounding in her head Anna felt
panic grip her at the thought of spending any time with
Ryan, alone in the house, without even Mrs Cassidy there
to act as chaperon.

'No, thanks,' she said curtly, already edging away. 'I'll
come back later.'

She had seen just that expression on his face then,
Anna realised, the same tightening of his jaw muscles
that drew his mouth into a thin, hard line, the way his
eyes had narrowed into slits in a face that was as cold
and hard as granite, and she felt a *frisson* of fear shiver
over her skin.

'Where would you like me to sit?' she asked, returning to practicalities in order to try to defuse the
almost tangible tension that filled the room.

With a curt gesture Ryan silently indicated the chair
set where the light from the windows would fall directly
on her face.

'Did you bring some clothes?' he asked, referring to
the fact that he had telephoned during the week to

suggest that she bring with her several different outfits
so that they could decide which one she should wear.

'Right here.'

Anna was grateful for the fact that she was once more
dealing with the artist, the professional, not the disturbing character of her memories, as Ryan sorted
through the clothes swiftly.

'Put this on.' He tossed a blouse towards her. 'The
skirt you have on will do—it's only head and shoulders.
You can change in the bathroom—through there.' A nod
of his head indicated the door leading out of the studio
and then he turned his back on her, becoming absorbed
in his preparations, selecting charcoal, brushes, paints.

The blouse was the one she would have chosen for
herself, Anna reflected in the privacy of the bathroom.
In rich emerald silk satin, it had a high neck and full,
flowing sleeves gathered into tight cuffs at the wrists. Its
colour was a perfect foil for the copper and gold of her
hair, and it seemed to bring her eyes into sharper focus,
making their mossy green seem clearer, stronger than
ever before.

'Leave your hair loose,' had been the last command
that Ryan had flung at her as she left the room, and so
now she simply ran a brush through it, added a slick of
bronze lipstick and an extra touch of mascara, and took
several deep breaths to calm her heart, which had un-
accountably started to race, before returning to the
studio.

It took some minutes for Ryan to arrange her in the
pose he wanted, changing his mind several times and
adjusting the way she held her head, her hands, the fall
of her hair, and for the whole of that time Anna felt as
if she was holding her breath, her body tensing in an
effort not to flinch away from him, even though the
touch of his fingers was cool and impersonal. She knew

from the way Ryan's lips compressed tightly that he had noticed her reaction and that it had angered him and her stomach twisted in apprehensive anticipation of his furious reaction, but to her surprise he kept silent until at last he stood back and nodded his satisfaction.

'I knew that blouse was right as soon as I saw it. Mind you, what I'd really have liked to paint you in is the dress you wore to the ball——' An unexpectedly warm smile curled his lips in sensual appreciation. 'You looked like Madame Recamier in that.'

Anna had to fight hard against an involuntary movement of reaction, praying that nothing of what she was feeling showed in her face. She knew of the nineteenth-century painting he meant, and the recollection of the subject's languorous pose on the thickly padded couch, the sensual effect of the draped shawl, bare feet, and the creamy flesh exposed by the delicate white dress, its bodice almost non-existent, made her feel distinctly uncomfortable. The woman in the painting looked as if she had just got out of a bed in which she had made love with the artist—which was not how she wanted Ryan to look at her at all.

And that feeling was made all the worse by the way that, as soon as Ryan started work—which should have been the point at which she could relax, knowing that his attention was concentrated on what he was doing— she found that she was once again a prey to the hyper-sensitivity which had assailed her on the previous occasion, when he had been sketching her.

Once more, the effect of those swift, assessing glances was like an actual caress, like the slide of the soft satin over her skin with every breath she took. She was also disturbingly aware of the firm, lithe length of Ryan's body in the navy, paint-stained T-shirt and denim jeans so worn that they seemed to have no shape of their own

but clung to the tight lines of his long legs and narrow
hips as if moulded on to them. The glossy blue-black
hair gleamed in the sunlight, and the strongly carved
face was totally absorbed, intent on what he was doing.
The movements of his talented hands, sketching swift,
confident lines on the canvas before him, fascinated
Anna, holding her gaze mesmerised as she watched the
play of muscles in his arms and shoulders, and unerringly her mind was drawn back to the night of the ball
when she had looked down on those powerful shoulders
and that dark head bent over her hand——

No! She wasn't going to think of that, not now. To
distract herself, Anna rushed into hasty speech.

'You said that your father had died; is your mother
still living?'

It was not perhaps the most tactful of questions, but
it was all she could think of on the spur of the moment
that wouldn't lead them into the dangerous minefield of
their shared past. To her relief, Ryan answered equably
enough.

'Yes, but she went back to Ireland two years ago. She
was never really happy in Yorkshire.'

'I know just how she felt.'

'No, you don't.' Ryan's tone was sharp. 'You know
nothing about my family, Anna-Louise.'

His pointed use of her full name stung like the flick
of a whip and Anna's pique showed in her voice when
she retorted, 'I saw you every day of my life for over
five years!'

Ryan shook his dark head firmly. 'You saw only what
you wanted to see—and hold still! I can't work if you
keep fidgeting about!'

'I wasn't fidgeting!' Anna protested, not liking his tone
at all. She wouldn't say another word, she resolved; she

didn't want to talk to the wretched man anyway. But Ryan clearly wasn't prepared to leave things at that.

'Don't you want to know about Rory too?' he asked with a satirical inflexion that infuriated Anna.

'Yes, tell me about Rory,' she said nastily. 'Is he still in the same...' she paused deliberately to give the word a sarcastic emphasis '...business?'

Only by the slightest flicker of a glance in her direction did Ryan give any indication that the pointed barb had hit home.

'Still taking things from other people's houses, do you mean? Yes, he still does that.'

Ryan's nonchalant way of speaking was shocking, all the more so when Anna recalled the meeting in the car park, and Rory's drunken declaration that this was his last night of freedom. How could Ryan be so casual about the fact that his brother was a thief—that he was in prison? Didn't he worry what other people might think if they found out? Probably not; knowing Ryan, she supposed that he didn't give a damn. Deciding it was wiser not to comment, she kept silent, but something in her expression must have given her away because she heard Ryan's sudden laughter.

'You're too transparent, Anna-Louise. Everything you're thinking is written on your face. It might just interest you to know that Rory now takes things from other people's houses with their full approval. He went into partnership in a removal business four years ago and he's doing very well. He's a married man now, too— as of the first of June, as a matter of fact. He was married here in London, where his wife's parents live— they're still on honeymoon somewhere.'

Anna found that her ability to form words had deserted her as she was bombarded by a storm of thoughts and feelings that made her head spin. Rory—the wild one of the Cassidy brothers—established in his own business, and married! The date Ryan had mentioned struck a faintly ominous chord in her head, and, thinking back swiftly, she realised that June the first would have been the day after she and Marc had encountered Rory— and Ryan—in the car park. 'My last night of freedom'! She had taken the words to mean that he was going to prison again, when they had simply been the traditional, joking description of the last night before he got married. He had been out on his stag-night with Ryan.

'Nothing to say?' Ryan enquired caustically. 'No, I don't suppose you have. Look, Rory's made some mistakes in his past—we all have——'

Hearing the subtle change in his voice, Anna tensed, unable to stop herself from wondering whether he was making an oblique reference to that last night before she had left Forgeley for good. And if he was, then exactly what sort of mistake did he consider it to be?

'But he's paid for them, and got his life back into order again. When he came out of gaol that first time he was determined never to go back. He worked hard, built himself a very different reputation—and luckily not everyone has held the past against him.'

There was no mistaking the way that last remark was directed straight at her, Anna thought, feeling her conscience prick her uncomfortably.

'I'm sorry,' she said hastily—and meant it, knowing that she had been guilty of prejudice, of jumping to hasty and inaccurate conclusions.

Ryan silently shrugged off her apology as if it no longer mattered, but suddenly Anna found that simply saying the words had sent her thoughts along a very different path.

If she had been guilty of prejudice where Rory was concerned, was it possible that she had been wrong about

Ryan too? Certainly, he had achieved far more in his life than her father had predicted he would. Edward Miller had been convinced that Rory was an inveterate criminal, someone who would never learn from his mistakes and who was destined to spend most of his adult life in prison, but time had proved him wrong, so why should he have been any more accurate in his assessment of Ryan? Privately Anna faced the possibility that her father might not have been a very good judge of character, and that, by accepting his judgements as gospel truth, she had probably blinded herself to his failings and prejudices.

But, no, disturbed by having to face up to her own lack of judgement, she was taking things too far. She was in danger of going to the opposite extreme of being too soft on Ryan. The night of Larry's funeral had shown him to be a callous, uncaring brute. That wasn't prejudice, it was fact, and it seemed unlikely that, in Ryan's case, time had changed anything. Wasn't the threat of blackmail he held over her—the only reason she was here—evidence of that?

Her thoughts kept her from speaking, and as Ryan, too, seemed disinclined to talk the next hour or so passed in silence until at last he threw down his brush.

'We'll take a break for a while. You must be getting stiff after all this time.'

'I'll be glad to move,' Anna agreed, stretching luxuriously in the warmth of the sun which streamed through the huge windows.

The sensual movement froze a moment later when, glancing up, she found that Ryan's eyes were fixed on her, suddenly so dark, they were almost black, and she saw the way that his hand tightened convulsively on the edge of the easel where it rested. Her heart started to thud so strongly that she felt sure Ryan must hear its heavy beat as she recognised the desire that flared in his eyes—recognised it and her own response as one and the same thing.

But a moment later the disturbing emotion had gone from Ryan's face, blanked out carefully, before he turned away, reaching for a cloth on which to wipe his hands.

'Would you like coffee?' After the intensity of feeling she had sensed in him just moments before, Ryan's casual tone sounded almost shocking to Anna. 'Or perhaps some wine?'

'Wine would be lovely.' Still stunned by her own reaction, Anna had to work hard to keep her voice under control. Perhaps the alcohol would relax her. Right now she felt as if her skin was tingling with pins and needles so that she couldn't have stayed still if her life had depended on it.

To ease the restless feeling, she wandered round the studio after Ryan had left the room, looking through the piles of sketches and canvases that were scattered everywhere. Some of them were completed, detailed portraits, others just a few brief lines, but all of them delighted her, filling her with admiration for the way Ryan had caught the spirit of his subjects as well as their actual physical features. She was studying one set in particular when a faint sound behind her alerted her to Ryan's return and impulsively she swung round to face him.

'These are magnificent!' All the restraint of earlier in the afternoon was washed away by her enthusiasm. 'They must be some of the best things you've ever done.'

Ryan deposited the glasses on a worktop before coming to her side and taking the sketches from her hands. As he studied them a slow, gentle smile curved his lips.

'That's Mona. With a face like that, I could hardly go wrong.'

Anna was in full agreement. The group of sketches, four in all, were of one person, a woman of perhaps seventy or so, who had obviously once been a spectacular beauty but whose face was now lined and creased with age.

'She's lovely, isn't she?'

Ryan's eyes swung to Anna's face, a rather stunned expression showing in their blue depths.

'I would never have expected you to say that. I would have thought you'd hate all this——' One strong hand indicated the lines on Mona's face. 'Aren't you trained to try to erase the effects of time, smooth out all lines, keep everyone eternally young?'

'That's not the way I see it. I want every woman— every man too—to look her best—for the age she is. That doesn't mean I want her to look like some seventeen-year-old model if she's nearly eighty. I don't see why anyone should worry about the way their face changes with age—the lines give character, a new depth; I mean, look at her——' Anna indicated the sketch Ryan held. 'She was obviously a stunning twenty-year-old, but she's an even more lovely old lady. Time and experience have etched themselves on her face and given it a new and very different sort of beauty.'

'Which was exactly why I wanted to paint her,' Ryan said softly, and as he spoke blue eyes locked with green in an intimate moment of empathic understanding and sharing that made Anna feel as if time had suddenly been suspended, as if the world had faded away so that there was just the two of them left in existence, linked by a very special sort of communication that needed no words to express it.

The sound of the telephone bell was a shrill intrusion, bringing them back to reality with a jolt, and before he turned away to answer it Anna saw her own confusion

and regret stamped on Ryan's face. Dimly she was aware
of him speaking to whoever was on the other end of the
line but his words had no form or meaning in her ears.
How could this have happened? How could she have
shared such a very special moment with a man she believed she hated and feared? She was still struggling to
impose some form of logic on the situation when Ryan
returned to her side.

'That was Gillie.'

Was she imagining it, Anna wondered, or was there
still a subtle shading of something in his voice, an
undertone that revealed how he too had been shaken by
their closeness—and regret that it had been broken? But
when he continued that strange note had vanished, his
tone businesslike and matter-of-fact.

'I'm afraid I'd forgotten that I'd promised to help her
at the centre tonight.'

'The centre? Gillie's youth centre?'

Still confused by what had happened, Anna's control
over her voice was not as strong as she would have liked
and she sounded much more surprised than she actually
felt. Perhaps if that special moment had never happened, then her thoughts would have fitted with her tone.
She had known, of course, that Ryan had actively sup-
ported Gillie's plans for the youth centre—after all, that
was why she was here now—but she wouldn't have expected him to be quite so personally involved in its activities. But, after that moment of unity and
understanding, she now felt that she would never be surprised at anything Ryan did ever again.

But now that unity was gone, destroyed by the
sharpness of her tone; she knew that from the way Ryan's
eyes narrowed, could sense his withdrawal as clearly as
if he had actually taken several steps away from her.

'Yeah—some of the kids are keen on painting and drawing, and I said I'd go along and give them some advice whenever I could.'

There was a distinct pause and Anna had the illogical impression that Ryan was nerving himself to say something important—an impression that proved to be purely imaginary because his casual, 'You can come along if you like,' would have needed no special effort to say.

She was stunned by the sudden wave of longing to do just that which assailed her, a longing so strong that it frightened her.

'No, I don't think so,' she said hastily. 'I'm really very busy—I was pushed to find the time to come here as it was.'

She must still be affected by that strange empathy, she told herself. She didn't want to go anywhere with this man—it had been bad enough having to spend the afternoon here.

Though that wasn't strictly true. Honesty forced her to review the afternoon and face the fact that, apart from the friction over the subject of Rory, there had been no real unpleasantness to upset her. And she had thoroughly enjoyed poking around his studio, when Ryan had given his time generously, patiently answering everything she asked. He had said that he wanted to observe her before he started work, but that didn't necessarily include responding to a thousand and one non-stop questions with more detail than she had a right to expect—and moments of dry humour as well.

And so, because she had enjoyed that time so much, Anna made herself add, 'Perhaps some other time,' to soften the force of her original refusal.

It was because she had *wanted* to go with him so much that she had had to refuse. That force of need had frightened her, making her feel as if her world had been turned upside-down and inside out, and she needed some time away from Ryan's disturbing presence to try to sort things out in her mind.

'When shall we have the next sitting?' she asked.

'You're still prepared to go on with this, then?'

Something about Ryan's response, the sudden darkening of his tone, the hard edge to his question, pulled Anna up short. She was letting fantasy run away with her, letting that one moment obscure the real truth, the facts she should be remembering. Her face clouded unhappily, all the light dying from her eyes, leaving them dull and shadowed.

'Oh, yes, I'll go on with it,' she said flatly. 'As you've made blatantly clear, I have to—I don't have any choice.'

'No, you don't,' Ryan returned hardly, and Anna felt a pang of distress, her stomach muscles twisting in fear as his tone made it clear that whatever unity they had shared earlier had been a temporary aberration— probably an illusion on her part. After all, she only knew what *she* had felt; there was nothing to indicate that Ryan had felt any such thing.

'Then in that case you'd better tell me when you want me back,' she snapped, the discomfort of her inner feelings making her voice hard and cold.

Ryan gave an exaggerated sigh, his mouth compressing tightly.

'You're not helping yourself, are you? It doesn't have to be like this.'

'What other way could it be?'

'You could try being friendly.'

'Friendly? To you?' She had tried being friendly to Ryan on just two occasions—and look what had happened then. 'I'd rather kiss a cobra!'

Those blue eyes became arctic and Ryan's tone was equally glacial as he declared, 'You look just like your father—with that ''It contaminates me even to be near you'' expression on your face. He was always so quick to put others down—which was pretty arrogant coming from someone who made such a mess of his own life.'

'Don't talk about my father in that way! I know you hated him——'

'You're very quick to fling these accusations of hatred around,' Ryan put in sardonically. 'But, as usual, you're totally mistaken. I never hated your father—though I have to admit that I despised him.'

'*You* despised him!' Anna couldn't believe the arrogance of the man. 'How dare you? My father was a fine, intelligent and very sensitive man who had more than his fair share of bad luck——'

'That's Edward Miller speaking all right,' Ryan cut in scathingly. 'That's the version he wanted you to believe; I saw something different—a man who'd had some knocks, true, but who just couldn't cope when things went wrong because he never really tried to *fight*, and who eventually got to the point where he ended up distorting his already poor judgement because he saw everything through the end of a bottle.'

'No!' Anna's voice was high and sharp. He couldn't have known that! No one could have known. She'd never told anyone about the way her father had finally given up on life.

'Still trying to hide from unpleasant realities of life, Anna-Louise?' Ryan's tone and his use of her full name seared over Anna's raw nerves. 'When are you going to realise that you can't keep running from such things?'

'I'm not running!'

'Oh, yes, you are—that's why you're here.'

'I'm here because you trapped me into it——'

'You're here because you *let* me trap you into it. You could have got out of it so easily—you still can. All you have to do is to tell Marc the truth.'

He made it sound so reasonable, as if it were actually possible, but Anna's mind reeled at the thought of how Marc would react if she did tell him. And the way Ryan had spoken about her father made things so much worse. She hadn't realised that he had known so much, that he could tell Marc *everything*, even the way her father had turned to alcohol when the pressures of his life had got too much.

'But you never will, will you? It's written all over your face. What sort of character is this man you want to marry? Why can't you tell me to go to hell—do my worst? Why can't you tell me that Denton wouldn't care?'

Because she knew that he would. Because she could have little doubt that Marc, who believed that she came from a comfortable, respectable background, would react very badly to the revelation that her father had drunk himself into an early grave in a shabby back-street house. And because she knew that such things would shock Marc so much, she couldn't tell him the truth as Ryan had defied her to. That fact had a bitter irony because it meant that she had to face Ryan's blackmail all on her own instead of being able to turn to Marc for help, as she should have been able to turn to the man she hoped to marry.

'You can't tell me that, can you?' Ryan taunted her cruelly. 'You can't tell me that this man, whom you describe as a perfect gentleman——'

'Which he is!'

'Is he, Anna? Wouldn't a real gentleman love you for what you are—not giving a damn about the past?'

Love. Suddenly the word sounded rather strange and disturbingly alien in Anna's ears, jarring her thoughts uncomfortably. *Did* Marc love her? He had never actually said so, but she had always accepted that as part of his natural reticence, his unemotional nature. Now she was disturbingly aware that such an answer wasn't fully satisfying.

'And wouldn't a real gentleman keep quiet about that past if he knew it could hurt someone's hopes of the future?'

She flung the words into Ryan's dark face, strangely unsettled by his use of that emotive word 'love' and her own reaction to it. When an uncontrolled part of her mind threw up the question, did *she* really love Marc? she pushed the query aside hastily, telling herself it was too stupid even to consider. Of course she loved Marc— she wanted to marry him, didn't she?

'Ah, but as you've been at such pains to point out— I'm no gentleman. And I'm not letting you off the hook quite so easily. If you won't tell Denton the truth, then the only way you can make sure he doesn't find out is to go along with what I want. It's your partner or me, Anna-Louise—there's no alternative.'

'It's your partner or me.' The words rang in Anna's head over and over again long after she had left Ryan's flat, and with each repetition they began to sound more and more ominous, as if Ryan's ultimatum was meant for the rest of her life, not just the length of time it would take to complete the portrait.

CHAPTER EIGHT

'NEARLY finished.'

Anna signed the last letter, added it to the pile on her desk and turned to smile at Marc, who stood by the large window in her office.

'There, that's done. Now we can go to lunch—oh, damn!' The exclamation escaped her as a warning buzz from her telephone told her that her secretary was trying to contact her.

'Yes, Alice?' she said resignedly.

'There's a Mr Cassidy to see you, Miss Miller.'

Cassidy! Just what was *Ryan* doing here? Anna prayed that the spasm of nervous tension that twisted in her stomach didn't show in her face as she turned an apologetic glance on Marc.

'It must be something to do with the painting——'

'Not at all.' The response came from the doorway, Ryan obviously not having bothered to wait to be invited in. 'I simply wanted to see where you worked—the nerve-centre of your *business empire*.'

Anna flinched at his tone, the sardonic emphasis on the last words piquing her so that she rounded on him sharply.

'I don't recall asking Alice to show you in!'

'No,' Ryan agreed with an infuriating absence of concern. 'But I knew you'd want to see me—that you wouldn't want me to stand on ceremony. Morning, Denton,' he added, his casual and belated acknowledgement of Marc's presence a calculated insult.

'Well, I can't talk to you now.'

Unease at that 'I knew you'd want to see me' stiffened Anna's tone so that it sounded hard and brittle. What if Marc took it to mean that there was more between herself and Ryan than the meetings which were necessary for her sitting for her portrait? Which was probably exactly what Ryan wanted him to think, she reflected bitterly. She should have known that simple blackmail wouldn't be enough for him—now he was tightening the screws a little, playing on her fear of the way he could destroy her relationship with Marc if he chose to, and enjoying watching her squirm.

'As a matter of fact we were just on our way out to lunch.'

'Oh, well, then I'll——'

'I can spare a few minutes, Anna,' Marc put in rather too hastily, obviously realising, as Anna had, that Ryan was about to declare his intention of joining them in the restaurant and acting quickly to forestall him.

'I thought you might,' Ryan murmured, the dark irony lacing his tone revealing only too clearly that he knew what they had both been thinking.

'Then won't you sit down, Mr Cassidy?'

Anna didn't want to say it; she didn't want to spend any more time in his company than she had to. But politeness decreed that she should at least make the suggestion, and she was beginning to grow tired of craning her neck back to look up at Ryan, who topped Marc's height by several inches.

Dressed in superbly tailored black trousers, a crisp white shirt and a cool grey linen jacket, and towering above her like this, Ryan was far too impressive a figure for comfort. Perhaps sitting down, on her level, he wouldn't have quite so much impact on her already decidedly frayed nerves.

'I thought we agreed it would be Ryan.'

A slanting, challenging glance was directed at Anna, defying her to contradict his words and the growth of a more friendly relationship implied by them.

This was not at all what she had had in mind, Anna reflected when Ryan had lowered himself into the seat opposite her desk, obviously comfortably relaxed, his long legs stretched out in front of him as he lounged back in his chair with every appearance of a man who intended to stay for some time.

She had been completely wrong in her belief that he would appear somehow less threatening, less imposing, once he was sitting down. Even without his full height, the strength and power of his lean body still hit home, and there was no denying the impact of the lethal combination of jet-black hair and blue, blue eyes. And, of course, she had no idea which way he might jump. He had implied that if she paid his price he wouldn't tell Marc anything about their shared past, but bitter experience had taught her that Ryan Cassidy could never be trusted, which meant that there was no way she could relax while he and Marc were in the same room.

That thought effectively rendered her silent so it was Marc who, clearly having decided that, like it or not, politeness decreed that he should at least speak to their unwanted visitor, cleared his throat awkwardly and spoke.

'Well, now that you've seen Nature's Secrets, what do you think?'

'I'm impressed,' Ryan surprised her by saying. 'It's a larger enterprise than I had imagined, but you've still managed to keep the friendly atmosphere of a much smaller concern. The shops are well designed too—the bottles and containers are very elegant. I can see that women would want to have them on their dressing-tables as much as they would enjoy using the products.'

Anna couldn't look at Marc. Some unerring imp of mischief had put that comment into Ryan's head, touching as it did on one of the areas of dispute between herself and her partner. He had openly opposed the plain, almost severe styling of the bottles in which their products were sold, advocating something much more fussy and flowery, more in keeping with his personal idea of what was feminine.

The trouble was that she couldn't look at Ryan either. Nervously she reached for the letters she had recently signed and began to flick through them, knowing there was nothing which needed checking but simply using them to provide some sort of distraction so that she wouldn't have to just sit there, knowing that Ryan had noticed the way she was trying to avoid meeting his eyes—and that he in turn was watching her closely, with God knew what thoughts forming in his mind.

'You're a Yorkshire tyke, aren't you?' Marc was clearly not prepared to pursue the matter of design any further. 'You come from Leeds or somewhere.'

'Forgeley,' Ryan returned laconically, and just hearing that name spoken in the long-ago-familiar accent sent a shiver down Anna's spine.

That 'tyke', and the rather condescending tone in which it had been spoken, had caught Anna on the raw, making her hand clench on the papers she held. Her father had always referred to the other inhabitants of Forgeley as tykes in just the same way and it had always made her feel uneasy even as a child. She had never shared Edward Miller's hatred of the north—it had just been Empire Street which she had so detested.

'It must be quite a change for you to be down here— it'll be a real contrast to what you're used to.'

'Aye, that's right.' Ryan lounged more comfortably in his chair. 'I've come down to the big city to make my fortune.'

'Oh, come on!' Marc protested, not catching the irony in the other man's tone. 'You don't need to do that! From what I've heard you're doing very well.'

'Well enough—the critics seem to like my work.'

'Well, at least your pictures actually look like real people—not like that other fellow who came from the same part of the country. What was his name? Lowry? All those silly matchstick figures—a child could do better—and those appalling mills.'

'There are a lot of them up north.'

'Quite, but that doesn't mean I want to have pictures of them hanging on my walls—though I suppose a Yorkshireman might.' Marc was too intent on putting forward his own opinion to notice the dangerous undercurrents in Ryan's tone. 'In my home I want beauty, not ugliness.'

'You want to ignore the realities of life?'

Once more, Anna caught the hostility that lay under Ryan's apparent calm like broken glass at the bottom of a still, quiet pool, not quite concealed by his smoothly polite voice, and the glance he slanted at her was filled with a cold contempt that had Anna bridling in anger at the realisation that he was including herself in his condemnation of Marc.

'Well—no—but I don't have to live with it! And you can't want to either or you'd not have got away from it all and come down here. There must be much more scope for a man of your talents in London instead of mouldering away up in Yorkshire.'

Ryan didn't bother to reply to that remark, but then Anna wouldn't have expected the man who had painted a series of portraits of tramps on the streets of

Manchester would consider Marc's opinions worth commenting on. She was grateful for the fact that her partner had taken just that moment to glance at his watch again so that he didn't catch the look which flickered over him, Ryan's bright blue eyes darkening with an emotion that made her feel cold with apprehension.

In spite of his stylish clothes, his urbane exterior, there was an untamed, primitive element in Ryan Cassidy that seemed alien and dangerous when confined in their present elegant pale blue and gold surroundings. Compared to Marc, he seemed like a sleek but fierce black panther in contrast to a pampered, well-fed pussy cat—a rather smug, self-satisfied pussy cat, she reflected uncomfortably, seeing the look on Marc's face.

'And of course you can command any sort of fee you want.' Naturally, Marc was interested in the financial side of things, and he seemed more at ease now that he had directed the conversation on to this particular topic.

'I get by.' It was a blatant understatement.

'You do more than that according to the reports in the papers.'

'You don't want to believe everything you read—some reporters will say owt they like to sell a story.'

'But you did turn down all that money to paint Pamela Curtiss.'

'That's ancient history.' Ryan dismissed the subject curtly.

'But why? Why didn't you want to paint her? She's a beautiful woman.'

'Oh, aye, she's a bonny lass all right. But I wasn't interested.'

End of conversation, his tone said clearly. I won't answer any more questions on the subject. Anna couldn't help contrasting his reticence now with the open and honest explanation of his decision which he had given

her on her first visit to his flat. Why didn't he just give
Marc his reasons? Because Marc would never understand or appreciate those reasons, a small voice answered
in the back of her head, and her partner's next words
confirmed that thought.

'But surely, for the amount of money he offered you,
anyone could pretend to be interested.' Marc hadn't
noticed, or didn't intend to heed the warning note in
Ryan's voice.

'I didn't need the brass.'

'But it would only have taken a few hours of your
time——'

Anna couldn't concentrate on Marc's argument because Ryan's adamant declaration had jarred on her
nerves, making her realise that something was wrong—
or, at least, very different. Was it her imagination or had
Ryan's voice changed since he had begun talking to
Marc?

On every other occasion when she had spoken to him
she wouldn't have been able to distinguish the way he
spoke from the voices of any of her male acquaintances,
apart from that faint trace of an accent. But now the
Irish lilt had been overlaid by a rougher, harsher emphasis, the vowels had broadened, and the man who
hadn't let slip a single dialect word in all the conversations they had had in his flat was suddenly peppering
his speech with them in a way that would have been
positively laughable if it had been used in some badly
written soap opera.

Anna listened hard as Ryan continued his conversation with Marc, concentrating more on *how* he was
speaking rather than what he was saying, and discovered
that her suspicions were right. The man who had had
little trace of a Yorkshire accent before was now laying

it on with a trowel. In another moment she expected him
to drop his 'aitches' as well.

Casting her mind back over the conversation, she
realised that the change in Ryan's voice had come about
when Marc had described him, rather condescendingly,
as a Yorkshire tyke. Clearly that had piqued him and he
was now playing with Marc, acting the sort of 'tyke' he
thought the other man had expected—and Marc didn't
have the faintest idea what was going on. With that realisation came a flare of anger at the way a lout like
Cassidy dared to mock someone like Marc in this way—
but mixed with that anger was an irrepressible touch of
amusement at his teasing and, it had to be admitted,
some impatience at Marc himself for the way he had
swallowed Ryan's blatant stage Yorkshireman act.

Impetuously she leaned forward.

'Tell me something, Mr Cassidy,' she interjected
sharply, meeting the full force of that bright gaze head-
on as he turned to her. 'You've talked a lot about
Yorkshire—but isn't Cassidy more of an Irish name?'

He knew she'd seen through his play-acting; a sudden
gleam in his eyes, a tiny upward quirk of one corner of
his wide mouth acknowledged the fact without words,
and suddenly Anna had to fight hard to hold on to her
anger, ruthlessly suppressing the tiny, irrational part of
her mind which was already responding instinctively to
the transformation of his face, acknowledging the attraction of that half-smile, the amused, silent admission
of the way he had been caught out.

'You're quite right. My parents are both Irish, and I
was born in a small village in County Monaghan myself,
and we moved to England when I was six.'

'So really one would expect you to have an Irish
accent.' Anna couldn't resist the dig.

'Accents are strange things, Miss Miller.'

Ryan had dropped the act completely, the rough-edged speech and heavy Yorkshire accent disappearing at once—and what better way of showing Marc just how he'd been conned? Anna acknowledged as she saw the other man's sudden frown, the dark flush of anger which suffused his face as, belatedly, he realised the game Ryan had been playing with him.

'They can be assumed or discarded as you like, depending on what you want people to think of you—if they're fool enough to judge you by the way you speak.' The pointed remark was clearly directed at Marc. 'But such things are very superficial. Take someone like yourself, for example——'

'I don't have a Yorkshire accent!' Anna put in sharply. That was one thing her father had always insisted on— that she should take care with the way she spoke, pronouncing every word correctly and not fall into what he believed were the lazy, rough ways of speech of those around her.

'Perhaps you think you don't. But anyone who knows the north would be able to detect traces of its pronunciation in your voice—and most people would be able to work out exactly where you come from.'

The cold gleam in his eyes was a clear warning against any further rash challenges such as the one she'd just made, and Anna's heart seemed to be beating high up in her throat as she wondered just how far he was going to take this line of conversation.

'Well, of course Anna comes from a very different area from you.' Marc was still smarting from the way he had been outwitted; it showed in his curt, unfriendly tone, the coldness in his eyes, his very stance. 'I understand that Forgeley is pretty rough——'

'You've obviously never been there.' Ryan managed to sound resigned as if this was exactly what he had ex-

pected. 'It's a very fine city—but the Churtown district
which is where we...'

His deliberate pause was just long enough to force
Anna's pulse-rate into a higher gear as she waited nervously to see how he would go on, and another of those
sidelong, slanted glances only added to her sense of
apprehension.

'...my brothers and I—grew up, that's pretty tough,
but it's home to me. I might have been born in Ireland,
but I'm a Yorkshireman, by adoption at least. That's
where I really consider my roots are.'

Belatedly becoming aware of the way she had been
holding her breath, Anna let it go as quietly as possible.
Another danger point had been passed, and Ryan still
hadn't said anything that betrayed her to Marc. Clearly
he enjoyed tormenting her by taking her right to the brink
of exposure and then backing down, playing with her
as cruelly as a cat with a mouse. How she wished she
could suggest that they leave for the restaurant, but she
still suspected that Ryan would offer to join them if they
did, and with him in this tormenting, cruelly teasing
mood she had no wish to risk what might happen if she
or Marc refused.

At that moment there was another buzz from the telephone and Alice announced that there was a phone call
for Marc.

'I'll take it in Alice's office,' he said hastily, heading
out of the room with ill-concealed relief. Ryan watched
him go, an expression of undisguised contempt on his
face.

'Impressive company you keep these days, Anna-
Louise,' Ryan murmured, and Anna hastily swallowed
down her own annoyance at the way her partner had
abandoned her.

'Marc's a very kind man,' she said stiffly, feeling caught in a cleft stick, knowing that she could never tell Marc just why she felt so abandoned, so nervous at being left alone with Ryan. And what made matters worse was the way that she felt as if every nerve-end was sensitised, raw and uncomfortable. She was far too aware of the lean strength of Ryan's firm body inside the elegant clothes, the undeniable attraction of the devastating combination of sapphire-blue eyes and jet-black hair for comfort.

'Kind!' It was a sound of contempt. 'Is that all the enthusiasm you can raise? I thought you wanted to marry the man! And tell me—are you *kind* to him too?'

It didn't take much imagination to realise just what was meant by that deliberately emphasised 'kind', and colour flared in Anna's cheeks in response to Ryan's sardonic intonation.

'That's none of your business!'

'It is if I choose to make it so.' The warning note in his voice sent a shiver down Anna's spine. 'Though I have to admit that I don't know what you see in him. Tell me, what is the attraction in a cold fish of a human cash-register whose vision is completely blinkered— except when it comes to money?'

'I couldn't expect you to understand it!' Anna's declaration had more force than perhaps was wise, anger getting the better of her sense of self-preservation. 'But, believe me, he's got a lot more appeal than——'

Her voice failed as she saw his face change, the flames of anger that flared in his eyes, the way his skin seemed drawn tight over his cheekbones.

'Than someone like me—someone who's not a gentleman?'

Anna flinched inside at the bite of acid in Ryan's voice but then suddenly, unexpectedly, his tone altered, softening confusingly.

'Tell me, Anna-Louise...'

Anna suddenly registered the fact that she had never realised how much she had actually hated the pretentious double-barrelled name her parents had given her until she heard it in that soft, dangerous voice.

'This blindness to reality—this refusal to see the truth, accept the world as it really is outside this cushioned existence that your partner suffers from—does it apply to his relationship with you?'

'I don't know what you mean!'

'Oh, but you do.' It came out silkily soft, every word seeming to shiver down Anna's spine. 'Why else are you so determined to play a part—pretend to be someone you're not? Can't poor little yuppy Denton take the fact that you've lived—that you had a life before you met him? What does he want from you? A wife—a flesh-and-blood woman—or one of those pretty pictures he likes to hang on his walls?'

'You've no right to talk like this!'

Anna wanted to spit the words in Ryan's dark, tormenting face, but, conscious of the fact that Marc and her secretary were only a few feet away, in the next room, she had to restrict herself to forcing them from between tightly clenched teeth, her green eyes flashing fury.

'And now if you'll excuse me Marc and I have a lunch appointment. Goodbye, Mr Cassidy.'

At least, she hoped it was goodbye. Anna had the nasty feeling that she'd got through this encounter more by luck than good management. She didn't expect that Ryan would give in easily and was frankly amazed when he got to his feet without a word.

But she should have known that he wouldn't let her off so lightly. Halfway to the door he paused and looked back.

'On second thoughts, I think I do know what you see in your partner,' he drawled, the sardonic emphasis in his voice making Anna flinch as it caught on her raw nerves. 'After all, he's your father all over again.'

'So what if he is?' Anna flung back. 'I can't think of anyone I'd rather he was like!'

But later those words, and the darkly questioning look Ryan had given her, were to come back to haunt her when, in the restaurant, she told Marc that she had received an invitation to Gerald and Tiffany's wedding.

'I'll accept for both of us, shall I?'

'Not on your life!' Marc looked as if she had suggested something as appalling as cutting off his right hand. 'I'm not going to that fiasco.'

'But he's your friend——'

'*Was* my friend,' Marc corrected coldly. 'If he's fool enough to marry that girl then he's not the man I thought he was.'

He moved the conversation into other channels, but Anna barely heard him. Looking into his smooth-featured, unperturbed face, she couldn't help contrasting his expression now with the frown that had darkened it a few moments earlier. One word he had used about Gerald caught on her thoughts like wool on barbed wire and hung there, tormenting her with the truth. 'Fool,' he had said. 'If he's fool enough to marry that girl.'

With a sinking feeling deep in her heart, she recalled the dark anger that had filled his face when he had realised that Ryan had been playing with him earlier. She suddenly knew that if the truth about her past ever came out Marc didn't care enough about her to forgive the lies she had told. What would matter to him was being made to look a fool in front of his friends; the affront to his dignity, his pride was what would trouble him most and that was what he could never forgive.

CHAPTER NINE

'CAN I see it now?'

'No.' Ryan's tone was adamant. 'You can see it when it's finished and not before. I've already told you that.'

He added a couple of delicate brushstrokes to the canvas in front of him then stood back, his blue eyes going to Anna's face.

'Do you need a break? I don't want you getting tired.'

'No, I'm fine—perfectly comfortable.'

That was a word she had never thought she would use to describe the time she spent with Ryan, but, surprisingly, it was how she had come to feel. Ryan the artist at work was a very different proposition from the dark, threatening monster who darkened her dreams and overshadowed her days. He was a complete professional who knew exactly what he wanted, but at the same time he had always shown a careful consideration of the comfort of his subject. In spite of his declaration that when he was painting time ceased to matter—and over the past couple of weeks Anna had become well aware of how totally his work absorbed him—he never made her pose for so long that she became uncomfortable or stiff, always being sensitive to her needs as a person.

'All the same, I think we'll leave it there—the light's starting to go.' Ryan surveyed his work through narrowed eyes. 'It's going quite well—another couple of sessions should see it finished.'

There was a strange note in his voice, something that sounded almost like relief, Anna realised, flinching inwardly as something seemed to twist in her heart at the thought. Shouldn't relief be what *she* was feeling, relief at the thought that in a couple of days, a week at the most, she would not have to come here again and could go back to her old way of life once more?

But, amazingly, relieved was not how she felt at all. Carefully Anna probed her emotions, trying to see what they really were, and found it surprisingly difficult to come up with an answer. Because the truth was that she hadn't hated the sessions with Ryan as much as she had feared. After that first sitting, Ryan had never again referred to the past. He had been polite, casually friendly, and most of the time his intense concentration on his work had meant that they had spent much of the time in complete silence. But at other times they had talked, covering almost every topic under the sun, and, recalling those conversations now, Anna remembered how stunned she had been to discover how much they had in common—and not just on the superficial level of liking the same films or type of music.

In fact, if the threat of Marc being told the truth about her background could have been removed, then she almost might have come to look forward to the times she spent at Ryan's flat, because, if the truth were told, she had come close to liking Ryan himself. Their talks had revealed him to have a sharp, incisive mind, strong principles—many of which she shared herself—and a generous sense of tolerance of other people's customs and beliefs, so that if she had never met him before she would have said that he was someone she very much wanted to have as a friend.

But Anna *had* known him before, and that fact threw a dark shadow over every moment she spent with him. Because of the past, knowing that that other savage, brutal side of him existed, she could never fully relax in Ryan's company. She still feared and distrusted him and so they could never, ever be friends because trust was a vital part of friendship and fear had no place in it.

Freed from the need to keep still, Anna stood up and moved to where Redford lay stretched out in a pool of sunshine. Kneeling down beside him, she began to stroke the cat's soft fur, letting her hair fall forward over her face to hide the disturbed expression she couldn't suppress.

'I saw Natalie today.' Ryan's voice broke into her unhappy thoughts. 'She looked wonderful—really happy. You did a marvellous job there.'

'It's what I'm trained to do. Beauty therapy isn't just about superficial glamour—cosmetic camouflage is an important part of the course.'

Her thoughts weren't really on her words, but going back to the time two weeks before when Ryan had repeated his suggestion that she visit the youth centre with him. This time she had agreed, and that evening had discovered yet another side to the complex personality that was Ryan Cassidy.

From the first it had been obvious that the children he worked with all adored him, and, after observing him with them for a time, Anna could easily see why. He was a brilliant teacher, able to explain techniques and approaches with total clarity, and at the same time communicate the excitement he still felt at seeing a painting take shape on paper or canvas. He moved among the group with a friendly word for everyone, offering encouragement, praise, advice when it was needed, and from the amount of laughter that accompanied his lessons Anna knew that the children were enjoying themselves every bit as much as they were learning.

It was then that she had noticed one girl of perhaps twelve or thirteen who seemed rather quiet and withdrawn from the rest of the group. She was a tall, slim creature with the sort of dark hair and delicate bone-structure that the top modelling agencies were always on the look-out for—but the fresh beauty of her face was marred by the fact that on her left cheek was a large port-wine-stain birthmark which spread down over her chin.

'Who's the girl in the red dress?' she asked Ryan when the class was over and the children were packing away.

'Natalie—one of my star pupils; she's gorgeous, isn't she?'

Anna felt a rush of happiness at the thought that Ryan saw past the birthmark, seeing Natalie as a person, someone who was beautiful in spite of her disfigurement. But then, after the way he had talked about the sketches of Mona, and other similar work she had seen, she wouldn't have expected anything else.

'Does that birthmark bother her? Do the others tease her about it?'

'I've had to have words with one or two of them—kids can be cruel about such things, and they gave her a pretty tough time. I really thought she wouldn't come back for the next session even though I provided a shoulder for her to cry on.'

'I—I could help her.'

Anna spoke jerkily, her heart having contracted suddenly at the thought of Natalie crying on Ryan's shoulder, his arms around her in comfort, just as they had been around Anna herself on that last dreadful night in Empire Street. At least, she had thought they were there to comfort her—she had very soon been bitterly disillusioned.

'The thing is, will she let me? These things can be a bit tricky—sometimes people don't want to be helped.'

'She's lived with the birthmark all her life,' Ryan said quietly. 'It's part of her.'

It was happening again, Anna thought, experiencing once more that feeling of sharing and understanding which had arisen between them when she had seen the pictures of Mona.

'Would she let me show her how to camouflage it, do you think?'

'It won't hurt to ask.'

Ryan had called Natalie over, and he and Anna had taken her to a quiet corner, where Anna had carefully tried to draw her out about her feelings towards her birthmark.

'I could show you how to cover it up if you like. There are specialist make-up products available that can conceal almost anything. All you need is to know how to apply them—they need careful shading.'

Natalie was obviously tempted but not fully convinced.

'I don't know what I'd look like.'

'Perhaps I can help there,' Ryan put in quietly, holding out a sketch pad on which, unnoticed by Anna or Natalie, he had been working as they talked. 'Is this the sort of thing, Anna?'

'Just the sort of thing.' Anna's smile was warm with genuine gratitude and appreciation of Ryan's sensitivity. The picture he showed them was of Natalie as she really was—but without the birthmark, her true beauty showing clearly.

'That isn't me!' Natalie protested.

Ryan turned that brilliant blue gaze on her face, looking deep into her eyes as he spoke with open, direct honesty.

'That's what I see when I look at you,' he said softly, and Natalie turned an excited face to Anna.

'When can we start?'

The camouflage had worked perfectly, Anna recalled, and Natalie, already interested in make-up, and with her innate artistic flair, had soon learned how to apply the creams herself.

'Well, you gave her self-esteem a real boost,' Ryan commented, bringing Anna back to the present. 'I hardly recognised her; she was bubbling over with confidence.'

'I was glad to help.'

Anna's response came vaguely, her thoughts occupied with more personal matters. She couldn't understand it. How could the man who had shown such concern and sensitivity over Natalie be the same person as the one who had treated her so appallingly? Sometimes the Ryan she knew now seemed light years away from the monstrous brute he had been so that it was almost as if he was some sort of Jekyll and Hyde character, and she had to force herself to remember the threat he held over her.

He hadn't mentioned that again either, but she would be a fool to think that he had forgotten it. He had given his word that he wouldn't say anything as long as she posed for her portrait, but now the painting was nearly finished—another couple of sessions Ryan had said. And when it was finished, what then?

'When is Marcus Denton's birthday?'

For a moment Anna did not understand the question; there seemed no reason for Ryan to concern himself with Marc, and she knew her confusion must show in her face.

'You were going to give the portrait to him,' Ryan prompted, a strange note in his voice.

'Oh, yes.' She'd forgotten that, forgotten that she'd declared her intention of handing over his work to Marc in order to shock him. 'It's at the end of September— the twenty-ninth.'

'Then there'll be no problem. The twenty-ninth is three weeks away; I won't need half that time.'

Something in her face must have alerted Ryan, because his expression altered and his restless movements—cleaning brushes, tidying paints—suddenly stilled.

'Is that still what you plan to do with the painting?'

Anna found it impossible to meet his eyes as she hunted for the right response to his question, not finding it easy to answer, even in her own mind.

'I—don't know.'

Could she do that? Could she just hand over the portrait to Marc? She'd said that was what she'd planned, her aim being to try to hurt Ryan by showing that his work meant nothing to her, but now she was no longer sure if she had ever meant it.

'Are you going to marry Denton?'

Quietly spoken as it was, the question still had the force of a blow, making Anna quail inside.

'Everyone seems to think it's only a matter of time,' Ryan went on, apparently oblivious to Anna's withdrawn silence, and the fact that she had not answered his question. 'The rising young businesswoman and the millionaire—it's thought to be a perfect partnership.'

Which was just how Anna had thought of it. Only nine short weeks ago she had celebrated her business partnership with Marc in the hope that perhaps one day they would turn that union into a more personal one. She had seen marriage to Marc as the pinnacle of her dreams, knowing that if he asked her to marry him she would have no hesitation in accepting. But somehow, in the intervening weeks, things had changed.

Unwillingly her thoughts went back to the day Ryan had come to her office, her own realisation about Marc in the restaurant later, experiencing once again the discomfort that the realisation of his shallow, selfish snobbishness had brought. Unlike Ryan, Marc would never have wanted to help someone like Natalie. He would have been repelled by her appearance, as he was by any flaw which meant that people did not match up to his over-exacting standards.

Belatedly it dawned on her that there had been a hard, strangely bitter edge to Ryan's voice on his last words.

'But you don't agree?' she said, lifting her eyes to his at last.

The sapphire-blue gaze flicked away from her to stare out of the window as if the shape of the clouds in the sky was suddenly of totally absorbing interest.

'It's nothing to do with me,' he said at last, and Anna was stunned by the pang of distress that twisted deep inside her at his dismissive response.

But then, what had she been expecting? Had she been hoping that he would advise her, tell her whether she should marry Marc or not? Why should she care what *Ryan* thought?

'He hasn't actually asked me,' she said slowly, suddenly needing to be absolutely truthful with him.

She saw his head go back slightly as if in surprise. 'And if he does?'

Anna wished he would look at her. It was hellishly difficult trying to hold a conversation with someone who wouldn't make eye contact at all.

'I don't think he will.'

Anna's voice was just a thin thread of sound because as she spoke she was suddenly assailed by such a wave of loneliness that instinctively she reached for Redford, cuddling the cat's warm body against her own as if by doing so she could ease the coldness which had encircled her heart. Her words brought Ryan's vivid eyes to her face in a rush.

'Why the hell not?' he demanded, and Anna suddenly found that she could voice all the doubts which had been growing in her mind for some weeks.

'You said it—Marc and I are partners, and that's really all he wants. We work well together, we complement each other socially, but a *partner*—business or social—is what Marc needs. He's not interested in marriage or a family. He's a workaholic; his work is what absorbs him, what he lives for, and I can share in that, and when he wants to relax—which isn't very often—he likes me there too.'

In the silence that descended as her voice died away, Anna thought that never before had she realised quite how spectacularly beautiful Ryan's eyes were. Looking deep into them now, seeing their clear blue softened by concern, totally without the cold, distant expression she had seen in them so often in the past, she felt as if she was being drawn out of herself, as if, like a flower responding to the sun, she was opening up to him, so that when he said quietly, 'And what about you? What do you get out of this relationship?' she knew that the only answer she could give him was the truth.

'I really thought I loved him, but there was more to it than that. With Marc I had security—acceptance. He was very much part of the sort of society to which I wanted to belong, he was my key to the door into the magic kingdom if you like. As his girlfriend, his partner—and perhaps one day as his wife—I was accepted——'

Belatedly she became aware that she was talking about her relationship with Marc as being in the past, and, seeing Ryan's frown, revealing that he had noticed it too, she faltered, unable to go on.

'And that was so important to you?'

'Yes! Oh, I don't expect you to understand that—you've never cared what people thought of you...'

What had she said to make the light fade from his eyes, his face close up so that it was clear that he had withdrawn from her?

'But I've never really belonged anywhere—not in Empire Street, not at any time since. My first memories are of always being on the move—away from Kent, to the north, from one house to another. And then my mother died and it seemed that, mentally at least, my father died too. Deep down, he didn't really want *me*——'

Her voice caught in her throat as she realised that this was the first time she had ever told anyone this in her whole life.

'With Marc I felt I was accepted—I *belonged*—and I wanted that so very much.'

'And if he'd asked you to marry him you'd have agreed—in order to keep things that way.' It was a statement, not a question, a ruthless undertone defying Anna to dodge the issue.

Wearily she nodded. 'I thought that if I married Marc I'd finally win my father's approval and leave Empire Street behind once and for all.'

'Oh, Anna!' Ryan drew a deep, uneven breath, pushing his hands through the blue-black strands of his hair. 'What are you doing to yourself?'

Suddenly he moved, coming to her side and gently taking the cat from her, putting his hands in hers. Surprisingly, Anna found that she didn't feel the loss of her furry comforter; instead, she was only aware of the warmth and strength of the hands enclosing hers, the mesmeric force of his eyes, the lean, lithe body next to her.

'Don't you see? You can't leave Empire Street behind. It will always be with you—a part of you. You can't erase your past—your *self*—as you can a pencil-line or a piece of shading that doesn't quite work. That's what made you who you are; it's *you*, and you have to accept yourself—then other people don't matter.'

'You don't understand!' How could he? He'd never felt that he didn't belong in his whole life.

'Don't I? Look.'

Gently Ryan drew Anna to her feet, leading her across the room to a cupboard which stood against a far wall. Releasing her for a moment, he searched through a drawer, finally pulling out a thick folder crammed full of papers, which he held out to her.

'Take a look at those.'

Bewildered by his actions and by the strange, uneasy, almost defensive expression on his face, Anna took the folder awkwardly and fumbled with the fastening.

'Let me.' Suddenly Ryan seemed impatient that she should see what was inside the folder, and he took it from her, pulling out sheets of paper and scattering them on the table near by. 'Look at this—and this——'

Anna stared in amazed confusion as painting after painting showered down on to the wooden surface like a flurry of snowflakes—landscapes, still lifes, portraits— dozens, perhaps even hundreds of them, all skilfully executed, but somehow strangely unsatisfactory. They were too soft—the landscapes of idyllic country cottages, the portraits idealised, sentimental, unreal. They were paintings without any heart.

'I don't understand——'

Then suddenly, looking up into Ryan's face, seeing the tension that drew his skin tight over his bones, she felt a shock of realisation, sharp as the burn of an electric current.

'Who painted these?'

She knew the answer from the way his face changed but still couldn't believe it.

'I did.'

'You——' Anna's eyes went back to the pictures, trying to see in them something of the magnificent power of his present work, the strength, the realism—the love that shone through even in the simple sketches of Mona. It wasn't there. Beside that blinding brilliance, these paintings were like the feeble light of a spluttering tallow candle. 'These can't be yours!'

'But they are—that's the point. This——' Ryan snatched up a pastel portrait of a young blonde woman, sparing it just one scathing glance before flinging it down again in a gesture of disgust '—this is what I was doing in Spain—churning out pretty pictures like this that made the tourists happy because they thought they flattered them; but they had no depth. They were the sort of thing you might like when you're on holiday in the sun and you've had a couple of glasses too much wine, but when you get it home it seems tawdry, like some kitsch ornament.'

'But——' Her green eyes wide above pale cheeks, Anna struggled to grasp what he was telling her.

'Anna, you said I didn't know how it felt not to belong—but you can't have forgotten that night——'

Panic flared in Anna like an icy flame at the thought that he meant the night of Larry's funeral, then died away as Ryan continued and she realised he was talking of something else.

'You were there when my father burned my paints. He couldn't understand that a real man would want to spend his life painting and drawing, and he wasn't having any son of his labelled queer by his mates in the pub or at the works.' Ryan's laugh was shocking in its harsh cynicism. 'I did everything I could to get him to accept me—I drank, I swore with the best of them, I always had some girl around——'

He shook his dark head in a gesture which combined disgust and despair at his own behaviour.

'And all the time I kept on painting in secret.'

Inside Anna's head a picture was beginning to form slowly, piece by piece, like a jigsaw—a picture of Ryan Cassidy as she remembered him, but the image was no longer the same. She saw the rowdy gangs of youths, the drunken homecomings, the fights, Ryan's endless stream of girlfriends—and, in the middle of it all, Ryan himself, morose, unsmiling, prickly as a holly tree, to her a constant threat, a source of fear. But now she saw that underneath the hostility had been his own private unhappiness—an unhappiness so much like her own—his fight to be accepted by his father.

'But then your father found out,' she prompted when Ryan seemed to find it difficult to go on.

He nodded slowly. 'You know what happened then—you were there.'

She'd told him she sympathised with him, but she hadn't really *understood*. She hadn't known what was at the back of everything; if she had, perhaps they could have helped each other then.

'So I did the only thing possible—I got out. I swore I'd never go back, and I really thought I'd found freedom at last. I went to Spain and worked in the fields by day, painting at night, and for a while it was perfect, but then slowly it dawned on me that something was wrong. My work had gone soft; it had no backbone. That was when I realised that instead of escaping I'd been running away—running from everything I believed I hated: Forgeley—the north—and all it stood for. But I was wrong. I *needed* it—it was my roots, my strength, my inspiration. I realised that I'd been denying an important—a vital part of me, and I knew I had to go back.'

And when he'd come back to Forgeley, he'd swept into her life like a hurricane, ripping it apart, shattering it into tiny pieces. But, even as Anna's mind flinched away from those bitter memories, something Ryan had said on that terrible night came back to her. She had asked what his father thought about the fact that he now earned a living by his painting, and Ryan had answered, 'He's accepted it. He's lost one son, he doesn't want to lose another.'

Only now could she see the full truth behind that laconic, throw-away statement—the fight Ryan had had to win his father's acceptance, the savage irony that that acceptance had come about in the end because of Larry's death and not from any true approval of Ryan himself. He had started to add something else, but she hadn't let him finish.

'You said that your father had accepted you, but it didn't matter——'

'Because I'd accepted myself. I knew what I wanted to be—I was a painter, but I was also a Yorkshireman. I knew I had to go back and live in the north, but this time it would be on my own terms. No one would tell me what I could or could not be—how to act, how to be a man. I was going to be *myself*.'

And he'd stuck to that resolution ever since. Ryan Cassidy made no concessions, put on no act, no matter who he was with. There was no pretence with him, no covering up the cracks, smoothing out the rough edges— he was himself, and that fact was reflected in his work, in the powerful, honest strength of the paintings that had taken the art world by storm. He was like his own portrait of the woman called Mona, with every line that life had given him displayed openly for the world to see, and just as those lines had given Mona a new sort of beauty so Ryan's refusal to hide anything about his life gave him the sort of deep-rooted strength that shrugged off any prejudice or snobbery he met on his way. Whereas she had trapped herself in the world of those prejudices, giving people the weapons with which to hurt her, confirming their snobbery by her denial of the past.

'I've never really been myself.' It was a cry of shock and bewilderment as, reviewing her life, Anna saw the truth. 'At first we moved so much that I was always having to adjust, never settling in. Then in Forgeley I tried so hard to be the daughter my father wanted—I couldn't mix with the other kids——'

'Did you want to do that?' Ryan cut in sharply.

'At first, yes. It was only later that they all seemed so horrible.'

Because by then, acting on her father's instructions, she had already frozen out any approaches of friendship. There *had* been such approaches, she realised. At the beginning, people had tried to talk, to help her find her way around—and Ryan himself had been one of the most persistent. It was only when her father had pointed out that his motives were probably not those of simple friendship and Anna herself had rejected his approaches coldly that he had become the morose, threatening character who had so frightened her.

But her father had not been the best person to listen to. Spoiled and cosseted as a child, as Ryan had said, Edward had never really taken responsibility for his own life, but had always blamed ill luck or someone else when things went wrong. He hadn't tried to fight, to get the best out of what they did have, but had simply given up and drifted for the rest of his life. He could have had friends in Empire Street but he hadn't even tried to fit in—and he hadn't let Anna do so either. Towards the end of his life, with his judgement blurred by alcohol, he had stuck to his rigid, prejudiced views, imposing

them on Anna too and so forcing her into the isolation
and loneliness which had marred her youth.

'Then when I left Empire Street I was so afraid that
people might not like me that I became the sort of person
I thought they wanted in order to fit in—and I've been
doing that ever since. You were right about Marc—he
did remind me of my father. I think perhaps I saw in
him the sort of person my father wanted to be—the sort
of person he would have liked me to marry. If I could
gain Marc's approval then, belatedly, I could become
the sort of daughter my father had wanted. But I never
really loved him; I just convinced myself that I did because I thought that was what I needed. I was pretending with him too as I did with everyone——'

But not with Ryan. Realisation struck home like an
arrow thudding into the gold in a target. With Ryan, she
had been able to be herself, never worrying that some
chance remark would catch her out, reveal something
she had tried to keep hidden.

'Ryan?' His name came chokingly. 'Ryan—who am
I?'

A gentle hand came under her chin, lifting her face,
and as her clouded green eyes looked into his deep-set
blue ones she felt the sense of despair ease away to be
replaced by a tiny seed of hope.

If *she* were an artist she would have loved to paint his
portrait, she thought hazily. His was a powerful face,
hard-boned, all planes and angles, so that most of the
time it looked harsh and unyielding. But now, with
warmth glowing in those vivid eyes, gentle concern
softening the hard features, it had a forceful masculine
beauty that stirred something in her heart, making her
feel as if something inside her that had been asleep for
years was slowly waking up, stretching, uncoiling,
coming alive. Ryan's fingers were warm against her

cheek, and his voice was as soft as a caress when he spoke.

'You're a very beautiful woman, Anna, and an intelligent, creative person. You're someone who cares about others—the way you handled Natalie shows that. You're an astute businesswoman—the creator of Nature's Secrets—but most of all you're *you*. You can be anything you want to be. If you want to leave Empire Street behind you, then that's fine. I might have gone back to Yorkshire, but I sure as hell wasn't going to live in Churtown for the rest of my life. You have to face your past squarely before you can move on from it; don't run away from it, accept it, then put it behind you. You mustn't carry it with you like some burden that will always weigh you down.'

Anna felt as if that burden had suddenly been lifted from her shoulders. She was on the brink of a new beginning and it felt wonderful, with a whole new sense of freedom.

'I'm me!' It was a sigh of release, of happiness, and Anna turned glowing green eyes on Ryan's face. 'Thank you!'

And then, because it seemed so right, because words were not enough, she stood on tiptoe to press a warm kiss against his lean cheek—and was stunned by his immediate withdrawal, the stiffening of his whole body in rejection.

'Ryan, what is it? Can't friends kiss one another?'

He closed his eyes briefly, thick black lashes lying like dark crescents against the skin that suddenly seemed stretched tight over his cheekbones, and when he opened them again their brightness was dulled, with a strange, dazed look about them.

'Friends?' His voice was husky, with a disturbingly uneasy note in it, one that made Anna react instinctively, putting her arms around his slim waist and giving him a firm hug.

'Yes—friends. We are that, aren't we? Only a real friend would have helped me see things straight, as you've done—and reveal his own private fears, pains, and mistakes to show me how I'd been going wrong. Only someone who really cared would have wanted to do that.'

The words seemed to hang in the air as she spoke them so that she could almost believe she could see them etched between them as the impact of what she had said hit home. She wanted to look at them more closely, consider the implications of what they meant, but the next moment all hope of rational thought was driven from her mind as Ryan muttered, 'As friends, then,' and enfolded her in his arms, bending his dark head to kiss her lips.

It might have begun as a kiss of friendship, and Anna had had every intention of accepting it as such, but from the moment Ryan's mouth touched hers friendship dissolved into something far more sensual, more enveloping and overwhelming. The tiny flutter of something stirring which Anna had sensed earlier now became a devastating explosion of awakening so that as her lips softened and opened under Ryan's she felt as if the force of what was happening inside her might actually shatter her into tiny pieces. The ground seemed suddenly unsteady beneath her so that she clung to Ryan, pressing herself close up against his hard warmth, adrift on a sparkling sea of sensation and longing, crying aloud in delight as his hands slid down her body, lingering tantalisingly at the curve of breast and hip.

'Anna-Louise!' Ryan's voice was a thick, roughened whisper in her ear. 'Dear God, Anna-Louise!' And with the words came a rush of bitter memory, echoes of those

same words spoken in another time, another place, which
slashed through the haze of pleasure clouding Anna's
mind so that she froze immediately. A second later she
wrenched herself from Ryan's arms though every nerve
in her body screamed a protest at the torment of loss
she was imposing on it, her mind just one raw wound
of shock at the thought that she had come perilously
close to letting Ryan Cassidy make love to her. She had
actually let herself forget what had happened the last
time.

Behind her she heard Ryan draw a deep, ragged breath
as if he was struggling to impose some control on himself,
and instinctively she tensed, anticipating the inevitable
explosion.

Amazingly, it never came. Instead she heard Ryan's
voice, rough-edged and distinctly uneven.

'Anna-Louise, what is it you're afraid of? Is it me?'

Firm but gentle hands closed over her shoulders,
turning her round to face him, her puny attempt at re-
sistance hopelessly ineffectual against his strength. She
saw the way his eyes narrowed swiftly, his deep frown
as he took in her ashen face and over-bright eyes, startling
against the rich copper colour of her hair, and suddenly
all the old remembered pain from long ago welled up
inside her, made all the worse by the realisation that only
a few moments before she had called him her friend,
had kissed him—forgetting how cruel he could be, forgetting his threat to blackmail her.

'Why should that surprise you?' It was impossible to
eradicate the pain from her voice. 'Don't you want me
to be afraid of you? Isn't that how it should be for
blackmail to succeed?'

She was totally unprepared for Ryan's sudden loss of
colour, the way his gaze suddenly dropped from hers to
stare at the floor, and when he lifted his eyes again they

looked strangely different. It took Anna several seconds
to realise that what had changed them was a look of
such uncertainty that she could hardly believe it was Ryan
Cassidy who stood before her.

'Anna—I want to apologise for that.' The softness of
his voice rocked her sense of reality even further. 'I
should never have done what I did—I had no right. I'm
sorry if I frightened you.'

Half a dozen replies, all of them scrambled and half
formed, whirled in Anna's head but she couldn't make
herself say any of them, responding instead with a
question.

'Then why? Why did you say that if I didn't pose for
you you'd tell Marc all about——?' she nearly said
'about us' but panic almost choked her and she hastily
substituted '—me?'

'I was afraid you wouldn't come back and I——' Ryan
seemed to catch himself up, and when he continued it
was with a subtly different emphasis. 'I wanted to paint
you so very much.'

'Me?' Because she was mentally thrown completely
off balance by this new Ryan, it was all Anna could
manage, and she saw his mouth curl into a slow, disturbingly sensual smile.

'As I said, you're a very beautiful woman.'

But he could paint a beautiful woman any time he
wanted. Any woman in the country, many of them much
better-looking than herself, would give their eye-teeth
for the chance to pose for him. Pamela Curtiss was a
stunner and yet he had turned down a fortune rather
than paint her. Anna couldn't convince herself that her
face had one quarter of the character of Mona's in the
sketches she had so admired.

'Not yet, perhaps.' To her consternation Anna found
that she had spoken her thoughts aloud and that Ryan

was answering her. 'But in another forty years, who knows?'

Abruptly his face changed, the light of amusement fading from his eyes, making his expression sombre and deeply serious.

'I'm sorry I behaved so appallingly, Anna. I just hope you can forgive me and I give you my word that you can forget that stupid threat—I never really meant it. I would never have said a word to Marc or anyone about your past.'

Not that it would have mattered anyway, Anna reflected privately. She'd only been fooling herself, believing that Marc would marry her. And even if he were to ask her, she knew that now she would have to refuse him because she had never really loved him either. She had only thought she did, deceiving herself because of her need to belong to the world which her father had believed was so all-important.

'Forget it,' she muttered awkwardly, suddenly a prey to terrible, tearing pangs of distress at the thought that Ryan had apologised for his blackmail threat but not the events of the night of Larry's funeral. Had they really meant so little to him? Had he really felt that she hadn't mattered, that any woman would have done? She had thought she had faced those facts eight years before but now they seemed suddenly so much worse, the pain they caused so much more agonising.

'Anna—can I ask you a very personal question?' Ryan's voice was strangely hesitant and uncertain. 'Do you and Marc sleep together?'

There was no escaping that searching sapphire-blue gaze that seemed to burn into her skin so that she knew he would sense immediately if she gave him anything less than the truth. But, anyway, she had done with pre-

tence. She had had enough of the problems that avoiding
the truth brought with it.

'No.' It sounded too stark, too harsh. She felt she had
to add something more. 'Marc's not a very sensual
man—he puts all his energies into his work and gets his
most intense satisfaction from that. And he never really
loved me—I wanted him to but I don't really think he
loves anyone——'

Her throat closed up suddenly so that she was incapable of saying any more. The truth was one thing,
but they were now on very dangerous ground indeed.

'And before Marc, has there been anyone else?'

'Since *you*, do you mean?'

Bitterness welled up inside Anna, seeming to burn
through her veins like acid so that she felt raw with pain
as she flung the angry words at him.

'You have no right to ask that—but I'll tell you
anyway. No, there's been no one, no one at all. I'm afraid
I don't subscribe to all the nonsense that's talked about
the wonderful fulfilment and happiness a sexual relationship can bring. It does nothing for me. My one
experience——' she spat the words into his dark, shut-
tered face '—was more than enough to convince me of
that.'

Ryan's expression changed dramatically, his face
whitening, and he actually flinched as if her words had
been the physical lash of a whip.

'Dear God, Anna-Louise,' he said in a low, shaken
voice. 'I never—oh, God, I was right when I said that
we still have one hell of a lot of unfinished business between us.'

CHAPTER TEN

'WHAT kind of unfinished business?'

The bite of anger still lingered in Anna's voice, but in the privacy of her own thoughts she admitted that her tone didn't accurately reflect the way she was feeling. Ryan had sounded so distraught, the ring of something that sounded like real pain in his voice, and through the darkness in her mind had flashed a tiny ray of hope that perhaps things had not been the way they had seemed. She didn't question why that should be so important to her but simply held on to it as a fragile lifeline, a dream of perhaps...

'I don't know—you tell me.' She had only heard Ryan speak this way once before; there had been that same lost and unhappy inflexion in his voice when he had first come to her side at Larry's grave. 'All I know is that for the last eight years I've had to live with what I did on that night, and I've hated myself for it.'

Abruptly he turned away from Anna, pushing his hands deep into the pockets of his jeans, his shoulders hunched as if against some intolerable burden. There was a long, taut moment of silence then he suddenly swung round again, blue eyes blazing in his colourless face.

'Where did you go? Why did you leave? I was away little more than an hour—just long enough to come to my senses and realise what an infernal shambles I'd made of everything—but when I came back you'd vanished. The house was locked up—in darkness——'

'You came back?' Anna's voice was just a whisper as she struggled to accept this incredible fact.

'Yes, I came back,' Ryan repeated vehemently. 'And damn nearly got myself arrested for trying to break down your door. I couldn't believe you'd gone—I was convinced you'd locked the door against me and were ignoring the bell, that if I stayed long enough you'd have to come down and talk to me.'

'*Why* did you come back?'

'To apologise—to explain.' Ryan shook his dark head violently. 'Not that there was any possible explanation. I behaved like a bastard—an animal——'

Days ago, perhaps even an hour before, Anna would have agreed with him unhesitatingly, but now she was no longer so sure. She had learned so much about herself and Ryan in such a short space of time that it had changed her perception of things irrevocably. It was as if she had gone through life wearing very dark, distorting spectacles, and now she had taken them off, seeing things clearly for the first time.

'There was more to it than that,' she said carefully and felt tears pushing against the backs of her eyes as she saw the dazed, uncertain look he turned on her. 'I'm here now, Ryan,' she went on softly. 'I'm not running away this time—why don't you tell me what you'd have said that night if I'd been there to listen?'

In those blue eyes she saw the flash of some raw, uncontrollable emotion that sent shock waves of reaction running through her, rocking her on her feet so that she actually took a step backwards to regain her balance, but a second later it had gone, and to her intense distress she saw his face change. It was as if a shutter had come down inside his mind so that she could read only rejection of her words in his expression.

Anna was totally unprepared for the pain that Ryan's reaction brought; unable to handle it, she rushed into anguished speech.

'Oh, Ryan—tell me, please. Tell me why—why did you——?'

'Why did I make love to you?' Ryan broke in on her harshly. 'Half a dozen reasons—none of them ones I'm at all proud of, and one or two that I'm downright disgusted with myself for. I was drunk, I was angry—I was jealous as hell.'

'*Jealous*?' All the times she had considered the possible motives for Ryan's actions, that emotion had never even entered her thoughts. 'Jealous of whom?'

Ryan's eyes dropped to the floor, avoiding her questioning gaze. 'Of Larry,' he said flatly.

'*Larry*? But he was dead——'

That brought those blue eyes swinging back up to her face. 'I know—I *know*——'

Because she had been there herself, Anna recognised the emotion that clouded Ryan's eyes, dulling their clear brightness, as the shadow of a terrible loss, one from which perhaps even now he was not yet fully recovered.

'He was dead, but *you* were there, breaking your heart over him. All you wanted to talk about was Larry—his was the only name you spoke. I'd always envied him the way he'd had the most beautiful girl in the neighbourhood trailing after him. He'd always been the one you wanted, and no one else ever got a look in.'

'The most beautiful girl in the neighbourhood'—'Ryan Cassidy fancies you'—'I've always wanted you, Anna-Louise'... Phrases from so long ago bombarded Anna's mind like bolts of lightning, illuminating previously darkened, impenetrable corners.

'I started out just wanting to hold you—to comfort you—but when you flung yourself into my arms all my good intentions went right out the window. I'd always thought I had more self-control than that, but——'

With a violent gesture, Ryan raked his hands through the midnight darkness of his hair, pressing his palms against his skull in a gesture so eloquent of self-disgust and shame that Anna wanted to cry out in protest.

Because Ryan could not take all the blame for what had happened. In the moment when he had said, 'You flung yourself into my arms,' it was as if yet another of those flashes of lightning had burned away all the bitterness and self-deceit she had hugged to herself for so long that she could see her own actions clearly at last.

She had not been blameless in what had happened between them. She had encouraged Ryan, inviting his kisses and caresses. She had kissed him back, and when it had seemed that he might draw away, when he had tried to impose some control on the situation, *she* had begged him not to stop.

'Ryan——' Instinctively Anna held out her hands to him but found that she was unable to go on when he grasped them tightly in both of his own, reaction to his touch searing through her like an electric shock.

'Anna, I know it's hopelessly inadequate—that it's too late—but I am so desperately sorry. I never meant to treat you that way. I—can you ever forgive me?'

Anna barely noticed that Ryan had seemed to bite off what he had been about to say and hastily substituted something else. All she could think of was the need to acknowledge her part in the events of that night, ease his burden of guilt so that he would know there was no need to talk of forgiveness.

'Ryan—it takes two to make love. You didn't rape me—there was no force used. I wasn't unwilling; I wanted what you wanted—our feelings were exactly the same.'

Seeing Ryan's stunned frown, she suddenly found that it felt right and completely natural to reach up a gentle hand and smooth away the lines of strain around his eyes.

'We were both lost, lonely, needing someone—and you were hurting like hell. You'd just lost your brother——'

A brother he had adored, she told herself, recalling how obvious it had always been that Ryan idolised Larry. Having lost her own father such a short time before, she should have been more sensitive to that fact. She knew only too well the feeling of devastation that could set in, the disorientating sense of shock, so that you couldn't think straight about anything. But her father had been nearly sixty when he died, a broken wreck of a man who had given up on life. Larry had been blasted out of life at only twenty-seven—and Ryan had only learned of his death because, by grim coincidence, he had arrived home on the day of the funeral.

'And you were understandably bitter because your father was so narrow-minded that he could only accept you as second best because Larry had gone.'

She saw Ryan's head go back, saw him blink hard in shock, and knew that she'd been right in her intuitive guess. He hadn't elaborated earlier, had simply said, 'I was angry,' but by taking that taciturn comment, together with all he had told her about his father earlier, Anna felt that she could better understand his feelings at the time, and empathise with the turmoil that had raged in him—a turmoil which she, unknowing, but also un-caring, had made so much worse by her own need for comfort. After all, wasn't that how she had felt herself, knowing that she was not the person her father wanted, that she could never fill the gap her mother's death had left in his life?

And there was something else, something which made
that empathy so much easier—and her need to express
it so much more important. Because in the moment in
which Ryan had said that his apology had come too late
she had known that he was wrong—that it would never,
ever be too late, that her heart and mind, which she had
believed closed against him forever, were now wide open
to his need for understanding.

Perhaps there had always been a tiny crack through
which he could reach her, though she had tried to seal
it off with the belief that she detested and despised him,
and that was why he had always been able to affect her
so much more strongly than any other man. She had
thought that she had loved Larry with all her heart, but
now, looking back, she saw that what she had felt had
only been an infatuation, a typical teenage crush which
her unhappiness and the stress of living in Empire Street
had turned into an overwhelming obsession. The truth
was that she had never really known what love meant.

But she did now. Looking into Ryan's drawn face,
feeling that she would do anything to wipe the uncertainty from his eyes, ease the tension in his taut muscles,
Anna knew that she had finally and irrevocably fallen
in love with Ryan Cassidy. Perhaps even on the night of
Larry's funeral, all those years before, she had sensed
something of the way she now felt, and that was why
she had responded so easily and willingly when he had
made love to her—only then she had blurred and confused her feelings by believing they were directed at
Larry. As she had done all along, she now realised.

Because hadn't it been *Ryan* who had had the strongest
effect on her during her time in Empire Street? She might
have followed Larry around like a devoted puppy when
he was home, but Larry had only been in Forgeley for
a few short weeks in all the years she had known him.

And in those other times, when Larry wasn't there, she had been constantly aware of, and affected by his darker, more difficult younger brother. Only then, not understanding the feelings he awoke in her, she had ascribed them to fear and dislike, just as she had done this time, when he had first come back into her life again.

'I want you to know that I don't blame you for what happened—and you mustn't blame yourself either.'

Anna's new awareness of her true feelings towards Ryan put a strong note of conviction into her voice—one that, she was glad to see, reached through to him, lightening his expression and making some colour return to his cheeks.

'There's nothing to forgive—no need to say any more about it.' Giving in to her overwhelming need to touch him, Anna reached out and gripped Ryan's arms, a current of delight running through her as her fingers closed over the hard muscle, felt the warmth of his skin. 'Please don't feel guilty about it any more!'

The last of the shadows cleared from Ryan's face, lifting her heart as they did so, but his expression remained sober, and there was no answering smile in response to the one that curved Anna's lips at the thought that he had understood and believed everything she had said.

'There's one thing I'll always regret,' he said slowly, 'and that is that you found the—experience——' his mouth twisted as he quoted her own bitter description back at her ' —so distasteful.'

Anna winced at the sting of self-reproach that came with the admission that she had used the scathing word deliberately, meaning to hurt. She had only found her initiation into womanhood so appalling because, still obsessed with Ryan's brother, she had believed that it was Larry she had wanted to make love to her, and that thought, combining with her inexperience, had destroyed the spiralling need Ryan had aroused in her, extinguishing it as effectively as if a bucket of icy water had been thrown over the flames of her passion. And so her body had closed against him, causing pain and disillusionment instead of the pleasure she could have felt.

But now, recalling the kiss they had shared only minutes before, remembering the feelings it had aroused, Anna knew that those flames had not been fully extinguished but simply lay dormant, like faintly glowing embers, needing only the slightest breath of air to turn them once more into a blazing inferno.

But *she* was going to have to be the one to make the first move because Ryan was still too shaken, too wary of hurting her to do so. Anna drew in a long, uncertain breath, her heart suddenly racing, and a feeling like the frantic flutter of trapped birds' wings starting up inside her stomach. She had never done anything like this in her life before and now, when it mattered so very much to her, she wasn't at all sure she could pull it off. How would she feel if Ryan did not respond or—far worse—rejected her? And how, added a nervous little voice inside her head, would she react if he *did* respond?

'We could always try again,' she whispered, the catch in her voice betraying her inner turmoil.

'We——?'

Ryan looked as if he hadn't been able to understand a word she'd said, and Anna knew a rush of panic at the thought that she might have to repeat her words, because she didn't think that she could bring herself to do so.

But then, 'We could try again,' Ryan repeated, this time with a very different intonation. His bright blue eyes were fixed on her face and she felt a nervous desire to bring her hands up between them to deflect that keen, searching gaze, protect herself from its probing force, because under its scrutiny she felt exposed and raw, as if every feeling, every emotion in her mind had suddenly been laid bare.

Please let him not ask why, she prayed silently, knowing she could never tell him the truth now—and possibly not ever. Ryan had been scrupulously honest— far too critically honest—about his reasons for making love to her on the night of Larry's funeral, but in all he had said there had never been a single word of love. He had made it plain that he had wanted her desperately— that he had always desired her—and that he cared enough to feel guilty about what had happened; but was that love?

Knowing that she had deceived herself about that emotion before, with Marc and, even more so, with Ryan himself, Anna wouldn't even let herself consider the possibility. If he had felt love then, being the honest, straightforward man he was, he would have said so. And if *she* were honest she knew that right now she was past asking for love. She wanted Ryan, wanted him on any terms, with no thought of the future. That would take care of itself; what mattered was now.

'Is that really what you want?' Ryan's voice was soft and in his eyes she saw the flare of a desire that matched her own, giving her the confidence to answer him with a new firmness.

'Oh, yes—that's what I want.'

If she had expected anything, if she had anticipated what his reaction would be, it was a fiercely powerful embrace like the one which had enclosed her on that night eight years before, but instead Ryan gently slid his arms around her waist, linking his hands in the small of her back, and drawing her slowly, ever so slowly towards him.

'We'll take it very carefully, Anna-Louise,' he murmured, drifting warm, delicate kisses across her cheeks, her forehead, the tip of her nose. 'There's no rush. And if at any point—any point at all—it's not what you want, then you only have to say...'

He paused, looking deep into Anna's wide green eyes, his own gaze suddenly very dark and intent.

'Promise me one thing, my lovely. If I do *anything* that upsets or frightens you, promise me you'll tell me.'

Already the magic of his touch was beginning to work. Anna could feel all her senses awakening to the sight, the sound, the feel, the scent of him. She seemed to be melting, her limbs becoming soft and warm so that it was an effort even to open her mouth to answer him. But the deep intensity of Ryan's voice told her how important this was and so she forced herself to speak.

'I promise,' she said and heard his sigh of relief.

'One other thing——' His mouth was very close to hers now, his eyes fixed on her lips, but still he held back. 'All those girls—in Empire Street—they were strictly for show, to impress my father with my masculinity. You needn't be afraid——'

'I'm not afraid.' Anna's voice was stronger this time, her confidence ringing in it. She was not afraid of anything where Ryan was concerned. 'I'm not afraid,' she repeated.

Only then did Ryan move to kiss her, his lips coming down on hers with a soft, undemanding tenderness that made her head spin and turned her bones to water so that she swayed against him on a sigh of pure delight.

'I think we'll be more comfortable in my bedroom,' Ryan murmured, his breath warm against her cheek, and Anna could only nod, feeling that the effort needed to walk the short distance was beyond her—she was only standing upright with Ryan's support.

As if sensing intuitively how she was feeling, Ryan lifted her bodily from the floor, carrying her out of the studio and down the small corridor which led to his bedroom. There, he laid her gently on the bed, sitting beside her with his arms around her shoulders, holding her close to him.

'All right?' he asked quietly. 'You're not——'

The husky note in his voice betrayed his uncertainty. Even now, he still wasn't sure that she wanted to go through with this, and the need to convince him put a new strength into Anna's voice.

'I'm fine,' she assured him. 'Just fine. Why don't you kiss me again?'

Ryan gave a small, slightly shaken laugh and did just that, but this time the gentle kiss and the softness of his caresses were not enough for Anna. Her body was coming alive under his touch, sending the blood pulsing through her veins, and his careful control was not at all what she wanted. With a small impatient sound, she nestled closer, linking her arms around his neck and deepening the kiss herself.

She could never have dreamt that a man could be so gentle. Ryan's touch was on her breasts and hips, as soft and delicate as the slide of the emerald satin blouse over her skin so that she barely knew when it was eased from her body and his hands took its place. But as she writhed her pleasure, intuitively sensing her need he let his caresses grow stronger, adding fuel to the fire that was growing inside her. The warmth of his skin against hers was a source of such delight that Anna cried aloud in joy, her hands reaching for him, her body instinctively arching against his.

'Gently, my lovely—gently,' Ryan whispered in her ear. 'There's no need to rush—we have all the time in the world——'

'But Ryan——' She couldn't believe that his self-control was this strong, that he could wait so long, putting her needs before his.

'It's all right,' his deep, husky voice assured her. 'This time's for you. This time will be perfect.'

And as she submitted to the sensual mastery of his hands and lips Anna knew that it *would* be perfect—it couldn't be anything else with her whole body glowing with sensation, the spiralling coil of need deep inside her so sharp, it was almost a pain.

When Ryan finally moved, sliding his weight over hers, there was a moment when she couldn't stop herself from tensing up, that long-ago memory slicing through the golden haze that blurred her mind, but Ryan soothed her with gentle words and slow, drugging kisses until she relaxed again, knowing she was in safe hands, that he would do nothing to hurt her.

What she hadn't expected was the sensation of over-whelming wonder as their bodies finally became one, her relief at the absence of pain turning rapidly into a deeper, more primitive flood of desire, pleasure piling on pleasure until she felt that her mind would explode with the strain of handling such sensation. And then suddenly there was no thought of any kind as she abandoned herself to the devastating white-hot ecstasy that made her feel as if she had been blasted out of her body and was floating among the stars.

A long time later, when she finally drifted back to reality, it was to find that, to her astonishment, her cheeks were wet with tears of joy, tears she had no recollection of having shed. As her breathing gradually became even again, and her heart eased from its frantic pounding, Ryan stirred at her side, lifting his dark head to smile deep into her eyes.

'That's what it's supposed to be like,' he told her softly. 'That's what should have happened eight years ago.'

CHAPTER ELEVEN

ANNA danced up the steps to the door of Ryan's flat and pressed the bell firmly, her foot tapping with impatience as she waited for the sound of his steps descending the stairs. The bright colour of her coral jumpsuit matched her mood and her heart soared as the door finally opened. She couldn't wait to see Ryan again; the last five days without him had seemed like an eternity, and she had so much to tell him. Her smile was wide and bright, directed straight at the face of the man in the doorway.

It was not returned. Ryan looked as if someone had slapped him hard in the face and she caught the flash of some more powerful emotion in his blue eyes before it was blanked out ruthlessly, leaving an expression that was worryingly emotionless and distant.

'You!' Ryan's tone could not have been more unwelcoming.

Anna knew that she had opened her mouth to speak, but no sound would come out. What had happened? How could things have changed so much so suddenly?

When she had left Ryan just five short days before, she had had to tear herself away from his restraining arms, forcing herself to go though it was the last thing she wanted to do, and only the knowledge that she had an important meeting with Marc to finalise the details of their partnership had persuaded her to go against her natural impulse to stay right where she was.

After they had first made love, she had stayed in Ryan's flat all night, and she supposed they must have slept—and possibly even eaten—at some point, though exactly when she couldn't be sure. It seemed as if they had spent all their time in bed, the delight in each other's bodies they had discovered unleashing a floodtide of hunger that seemed impossible to assuage. When she had finally and reluctantly realised that she would have to go, Ryan had tried to dissuade her, using kisses and caresses as well as words to keep her with him so that she had almost been persuaded to get back into bed with him before she had dragged herself away.

So what had happened to change all that? She had anticipated this moment with such happiness, expecting to be gathered into Ryan's arms, hugged until she felt her bones would break, and kissed almost senseless the moment he saw her. Instead, it seemed as if a cold, unyielding stranger stood before her, his face hard as granite, his eyes just blue chips of ice. In her heart she had known that their lovemaking would not have meant so much to Ryan as it did to her, but she had never expected this swift and total withdrawal.

'What do you want?'

Anna's mind went blank. The only thing she could think of was the fact that the last time she had been at Ryan's flat—before the course of events had changed so dramatically—he had suggested that they meet on Friday for one last sitting.

'I thought you were going to finish my portrait today.' High and tight with tension, her voice sounded almost as cold as his own.

'So I did.' But Ryan still seemed unwilling to let her in, holding the door half closed, like a barrier against her.

'Ry?' A woman's voice floated down the stairwell. 'What on earth's keeping you?'

So now she knew. Anna had to fight hard to keep from revealing how much the realisation that Ryan had another woman with him had affected her.

'You've got a visitor,' she said hastily, the struggle to keep her emotions hidden stiffening her lips so that the words came out harshly. 'Perhaps another time——'

'No.' Suddenly Ryan seemed to have come to some decision. 'You might as well come in.' She could hardly have had a more unwelcoming invitation. 'There's someone I'd like you to meet.'

Her mind a whirl of confusion, Anna followed him up the stairs and into the airy living-room, stopping dead in shock as she came face to face with the woman who was perched on one arm of the settee.

'This is Maeve,' Ryan said from behind her, and suddenly Anna knew exactly what had gone wrong.

She had forgotten about Maeve, the woman who had given Redford his name. She had forgotten the warmth in Ryan's voice when he spoke of her. Now her stomach lurched queasily and there was a sour taste in her mouth as full realisation set in.

It couldn't have happened a second time! She couldn't have been so terribly, foolishly, blindly naïve as to let Ryan Cassidy use her all over again! She had really thought that he cared—that, if he didn't actually love her as she loved him, then at least he felt *something*. But what sort of man could make love to her with such passion, knowing that in a few days his mistress would be joining him?

But she had pushed Ryan into it. *She* had been the one to suggest—to insist that he made love to her. 'Ryan Cassidy fancies you...' He had always found her desirable, and so, when she had foolishly given him the opportunity, he had grasped at his chance to have what he wanted—but it had meant nothing at all. Through a blur of pain she made herself take the hand that Maeve had proffered in greeting.

'It's nice to meet you,' some automatic little part of her brain forced her to murmur though it was in fact the opposite of the truth. 'Ryan's told me about you—didn't you name his cat?'

Instinctive self-defence made her speak as if the fact were a vague memory, not one she recalled with painful clarity.

'That's right. Perhaps Redford's a bit fanciful, but, left to himself, Ry would probably have lumbered the poor creature with Ginger or something equally original.'

Maeve was not at all as she had imagined, Anna admitted. In the Empire Street days, Ryan had had a noticeable penchant for tall, slim blondes, and this woman was at least five inches shorter than her own five-foot-eight, her hair was a rich, fiery red, and she was definitely on the large size where her figure was concerned. But it suited her, her generous size going with her warm, open face, the full mouth that looked as if it often smiled. And Maeve clearly wasn't ashamed of being much larger than was currently fashionable, wearing her vivid green and gold dress with the panache of a woman who had her own personal sense of style. She might not be conventionally beautiful, but Anna could well see how Ryan could be attracted to her. And she could be in no doubt about that, she admitted miserably, seeing the look Maeve turned on him, the sort of look that was only shared by two people who were very close, and Ryan's answering smile—the first to warm his face since her own arrival.

'Aren't you going to introduce me?' A deeper, masculine voice spoke from behind Anna, making her spin round sharply, the sudden movement betraying how much on edge she was.

'*Larry*?' The name came out on a choking gasp even though she knew it to be impossible. But then her mind cleared and she realised that there was only one person this could be.

'You remember my brother Rory?' Ryan said, confirming her thoughts.

Rory Cassidy lacked perhaps a couple of inches of his brother's slim height, but he made up for that in his strong build, being broader than Ryan at the chest and shoulders, and his eyes were the green she remembered Larry's as being, his hair touched by the same rich auburn tint.

'This is Anna Miller——'

Not Anna-Louise, or even the Annie Rory might perhaps have remembered better, Anna noted. Clearly, Ryan had already talked to his brother about her, explaining who she was.

'I remember.'

There was a disturbing note in Rory Cassidy's voice, one that made Anna feel distinctly uneasy, and his eyes held no warmth as, unlike Maeve, he kept his hands down at his sides. She felt as if she had wandered from safe, firm land into a treacherous quicksand, and the trouble was that she didn't know how it had happened.

'Rory and his wife spent last night here.' Ryan seemed to feel obliged to make the explanation though Anna thought that if she heard one more word in that carefully polite but distant voice she would scream out loud. 'They're on their way back home after their honeymoon.'

'Oh, yes, I'd heard that you'd recently married—congratulations.' In spite of her efforts to control it, her voice was tight with tension, cracking in the most embarrassing way. 'Is your wife here now?' Anna asked, and heard Maeve's rich chuckle.

'I most certainly am!'

'Oh!' Anna knew her confusion must show on her face as hot colour washed her cheeks. 'I'm sorry—I didn't realise——'

'Don't tell me you thought I was with *Ryan*?'

Maeve laughed as she spoke, but her grey eyes were fixed too closely on Anna's face for comfort, and Anna had the disturbing feeling that the other woman was watching her closely, looking for something—but what?

'I love my brother-in-law very much, but this rogue is the one I married.'

Maeve's arms slid round Rory's waist as she spoke, and for the first time Anna noticed the thick gold band on her left hand. Suddenly the raised colour left her face, leaving it pale with concern. If it hadn't been Maeve's presence here which had made Ryan withdraw from her, then she had no idea what could possibly have caused his coldness. The doubts that the belief that Maeve was Ryan's girlfriend had put into her mind still lingered, and pain tore at her as she considered the possibility that perhaps, after all, her father had been right, and once Ryan had got what he wanted from her he had cast her off like a discarded toy.

'Anna's here for the last sitting for her portrait. I'd forgotten that we arranged it for today.'

Ryan's tone told Anna only too clearly that he had done no such thing, but was simply claiming to have done so in order to upset her, which he had succeeded in doing—very much. The temptation to round on him, demand to know what was happening, was almost overwhelming, but at the same time Anna knew that she didn't have the courage to do it. If their affair—for she supposed that was what she must term their one brief passionate night together—were over, then she couldn't bring herself to force Ryan to actually say so here, in front of his brother and Maeve.

'But you're obviously busy——' she began hastily, and was surprised to find herself interrupted by Maeve.

'Not at all. Don't rush off because of us. Ryan—why don't you make us all some coffee?'

Something in the way the other woman spoke made Anna suspect that she was trying to get Ryan out of the way, and evidently he thought so too.

'I don't think——' he began, but Maeve wouldn't let him finish.

'*Coffee*, Ryan,' she said firmly, pushing him in the direction of the door. 'Rory and I will entertain your guest for you.'

Glancing at Rory's dark, unsmiling face, Anna suddenly had the irrational feeling that she would rather be in the kitchen with Ryan, hostile and distant as he was, and her suspicions were confirmed by the way that, as soon as his brother had left the room, Rory rounded on her.

'Why the hell are you here?' he demanded, clearly only keeping himself from shouting because he might be heard from the kitchen. 'Why are you doing this to my brother again?'

'Again? Doing what? I don't understand.'

'I think you do! You messed up his life once before—now you're doing it again and I want to know why. Does it give you some sort of perverse thrill to know that you can twist him round your little finger?'

Rory had to be crazy. Anna couldn't imagine anyone less likely to be twisted round anyone's finger—particularly hers—than Ryan in his present mood.

'I don't know what you're talking about!'

'Don't give me that!' Black scorn sounded in Rory's voice. 'You know very well what you're doing! Eight years ago, I thought that perhaps you were just a blind little fool, too young and stupid, too dominated by your father to know any better—but this time——'

'Will you please tell me what you're talking about?'

'I think we'd better sit down,' Maeve's voice broke in on them, her tone quietly controlled. 'Rory, love, at least give her a chance to explain,' she went on as Anna sank down on to one settee, and, after a few moments' hesitation, Ryan's brother followed suit.

'I don't even know what you're accusing me of,' Anna said after a few seconds' uncomfortable silence. 'What am I supposed to have done?'

'What——?' Rory began furiously, then, after a quelling glance from his wife, he clamped down hard on his temper again. 'You've been stringing Ry along, pretending that you care for him, then as soon as you get him where you want him you can't be seen for dust— just like the last time——'

'What last time?' Anna felt desperation grip her. She couldn't make head or tail out of what Rory was saying. She only knew that the accusations he was flinging at her fitted Ryan's behaviour much more than her own.

'Eight years ago, damn it!' Rory couldn't contain his temper any longer. 'And for a long time before that. You knew Ryan was crazy about you——'

'*Ryan*?' Anna's disbelief sounded in her voice. 'Ryan wasn't——'

'Oh, yes, he was. I knew it, Larry knew it—the whole damn street knew it; you must have known it! And so you took a great delight in making it plain that you wanted nothing to do with him. You cut him dead every time he tried to speak to you, laughed in his face when he asked you out—you wouldn't even sit in the same room as him unless Larry was there. And you flaunted your obsession with Larry just to rub his nose in it.'

'I never—you've got it all wrong——'

'You saw only what you wanted to see.' Anna's voice failed her as Ryan's voice sounded in her head, forcing her to look back at those days in Empire Street, recalling how it had been Ryan who had tried to talk to her, Ryan who had helped her find her way about, Ryan who had always told her when Larry was due home—Ryan who had been the only one to use her proper name. Influenced by her father's opinions, she had thought that he was just making a nuisance of himself, tormenting her like some of the others, and she had taken his offers of a date in much the same way, rejecting them coldly and swiftly because she had wanted to be rid of his attentions and feared that he might take a gentler refusal as some sort of encouragement.

'*Ryan*?' she said, this time with a very different intonation.

Rory was pulling something from his pocket, and now he tossed it towards her.

'Open it,' he commanded as Anna stared in bewilderment at the small, battered sketch book in her lap.

Her sense of shock grew as she turned the pages, seeing on every one of them a portrait of herself, hasty pencil sketches, occasionally shaded in with pastels: herself at thirteen, still just a child, growing into a coltish, long-legged teenager, and all the other years she had spent in Empire Street—and all stamped with Ryan's distinctive personal style.

'Ryan Cassidy fancies you.' The old taunt rang in her head, taking on a whole new meaning. And all the girls whom Ryan had dated—all tall, slim blondes, all very much her type.

'I didn't know.'

'You must have done. Who do you think protected you from the worst of the teasing—the real hassle you might have had?'

'That was Larry,' Anna said uncertainly, reading something of the truth in Rory's face.

'Larry!' It was a snort of contempt. 'You really were blind! Oh, sure, he muscled in once, but the next day he was back at barracks, and not even Larry could have helped you from there. It was Ry who made sure everyone knew that if they touched you again they'd have him to answer to. You wouldn't give him the time of day, but he'd always been there for you if you needed him. Mam told me that even after Larry's funeral all he could think about was how it would have devastated you, and he insisted on going to see you.'

Anna felt as if all her feelings had gathered into a tight knot in her throat so that she couldn't speak a word. She had thought that Ryan had found her by accident, but now it seemed that he had actually come looking for her.

'Do you know how he felt when you ran away that time? Mam said he was like a crazy man—she'd never seen anyone so desperate. He spent weeks looking for you, trying everything he could think of to find you. She was afraid he'd have a complete breakdown—he didn't eat, didn't sleep. It took him ages to recover from that—and then you swan back into his life all over again, like some vicious black-widow spider all ready to devour her lover—and when he's well and truly caught up in your web you drop him without so much as a goodbye.'

'Drop him?' Anna could only echo the words dazedly. 'I didn't—I——'

'You love him.' It was Maeve who spoke, and only now did Anna become aware of the fact that Rory's wife had been a silent spectator all this time, her eyes on Anna's face, watching every play of emotion across it so that she now spoke with complete conviction.

Anna could only nod silently in response, unable even to form a single word of agreement.

'You——!'

'Then why don't you tell him?' Maeve's quiet voice cut across her husband's blustering indignation. 'Can't you see that the poor devil's eating his heart out for you?'

Was he? Anna's own heart leapt at the thought that Maeve might actually be right, but then plummeted down again rapidly as she recalled the look on Ryan's face when he had opened the door. He had looked as if he hated her, as if love was the furthest thing from his thoughts. But if—as Rory had said—for some reason he believed that *she* had walked out on *him* ...

Suddenly Maeve moved, getting to her feet and pulling her husband up with her.

'Rory and I have to go out,' she declared, silencing Rory's protest with an imperious gesture and a hasty, 'It'll be all right—you should stay and talk to Ryan.'

And before Anna could say anything they had gone, leaving her a prey to a devastating mixture of bewilderment, a tiny, weak thread of hope, and something perilously close to blind panic. Any minute now, Ryan would come back into the room, and she didn't have the faintest idea what she was going to say to him.

Did Ryan love her? Rory and Maeve seemed convinced that he did—but Ryan had never spoken of any such emotion. And why should he believe that she had walked out on him?

Her heart seemed to leap high up in her throat as the door opened and Ryan appeared, a tray in his hands. He stopped dead as he realised that she was the only person in the room.

'Where are Rory and Maeve?'

'They—had to go out.'

'Out?' Ryan looked down at the tray and the four mugs on it. 'But——'

Suddenly he moved into the room, slamming the tray down on to the table with such force that Anna shrank back in her seat.

'What the hell's going on?'

'I don't know.'

Anna wished desperately that she wasn't sitting down; Ryan seemed to tower over her, dark and threatening. But she knew that her legs would not support her if she tried to stand up.

'Maeve said we had to talk,' she tried nervously.

'Talk!' Ryan's cynical exclamation lashed at her like a whip. 'What is there to talk about? You got what you wanted—— '

His dismissive shrug hurt more than the bitter anger she could see in his eyes, etched into the white lines around his nose and mouth.

'What are you talking about, Ryan? What do you mean I got what I wanted?'

Sapphire-blue eyes blazed into her confused green ones so that she felt they might actually have the power of lasers and burn her up where they rested.

'You had your fling—a sordid sexual episode—exactly what you wanted. What was it, Anna? Was it because, by your own admission, Marc was too involved with his work and you needed an outlet for the appetite he never fed? Or was it just for revenge? I suppose I served your purpose as well as anyone else—after all, I'm just a bit of rough—a back-street lout with no finer feelings——'

'*No!*' Desperation gave Anna the strength to get to her feet, her hands reaching out to grasp his arms, shaking them hard as if she could physically force him to see the truth. 'It wasn't like that at all! I tried to phone you but you weren't in. Didn't you get my message?'

'Your message?'

For a moment Ryan was completely still, and Anna thought she could see light at the end of the tunnel. If Gillie hadn't told him—if she hadn't passed on the message; after all, she was notoriously vague about details. But the next moment that hope was shattered as Ryan rounded on her savagely.

'Oh, yes, I got your message!' With a violent movement he wrenched himself free, taking several strides away from her. '"Tell Ryan I've one last piece of unfinished business *to get out of my system*."'

Something seemed to explode inside Anna's brain and her hand went to her mouth in a gesture of shock and stunned horror. Things had happened so fast on Monday that she hadn't had time to think clearly, and after trying to phone Ryan several times and getting no answer she had called Gillie, knowing that the other woman would see him at the centre that night. For her own private reasons she hadn't wanted to tell him exactly where she was going, so she had made her message deliberately vague, but now, too late, she could see how Ryan could have misinterpreted it—and if he had taken it the wrong way then it must mean that he was over-sensitive to everything where she was concerned—and the possible repercussions from that were more than she dared to contemplate at the moment.

'I didn't mean it the way you've taken it! I didn't mean that I'd got *you* out of my system. It wasn't like that.'

'Wasn't it?' Ryan's voice was a low, dangerous snarl. 'It looked that way to me. One night you gave me—*one night*—then you disappear just as you did the last time.'

And the last time she'd run away from him he'd gone searching for her, Rory had said, bringing himself close to a breakdown. Had he done the same this time? Did that explain where he'd been every night when she'd tried to phone him from her hotel? So was that anger in his eyes or the raw pain of a man who had thought that he'd lost the woman he loved for the second time?

'Ryan——' she began hesitantly, but Ryan didn't appear to have heard her.

'I've got something for you——' Swinging away, he yanked open a drawer in the desk and pulled out a small slip of paper, thrusting it at Anna, carefully keeping his distance. 'You can keep it as a souvenir.'

It was a photograph. Anna's eyes misted and her lips curved softly as she stared into the grinning face of Larry Cassidy.

'He doesn't look half as godlike as I remember him,' she said quietly, and sensed rather than saw the way Ryan's head turned towards her, his attention caught. 'But then, of course, at fifteen—sixteen—I was hellishly naïve. I had an almighty schoolgirl's crush on Larry and that made me blind to anyone else.'

He was still listening intently. Would he see what she was trying to say and, more important, would he let her take it further? Ryan's silence, his sudden stillness, the frown between his brows gave her some hope that he would and, drawing a deep breath, she forced herself to go on.

'Rory showed me some pictures too——' A wave of her hand indicated the sketch book still lying on the settee, and as Ryan's eyes went to it his sudden loss of colour made her heart lurch in a rush of hope that Rory had been right.

'He said that you—loved me—but because of my father and because I was obsessed with Larry I never saw it. I think I must have been terribly unkind to you without realising it.'

Ryan's swiftly indrawn breath and the way his hand made a sudden involuntary movement before clenching into a fist at his side spoke of his state of mind more eloquently than any words.

'Is that true, Ryan? Was I really so much of a fool? Was Rory right—did you love me then?'

For a long, long moment she thought that he wasn't going to answer her, but then his taut shoulders slumped in a gesture of surrender.

'Yes,' he said curtly, aggressively. 'Yes, I loved you.' The blue eyes defied her to take the matter further. 'Does that give you a thrill? Does it add to your enjoyment of slumming with a rough from Empire Street to think that he actually had the audacity to fall in love with you?'

'Oh, Ryan.' Anna's voice was soft, but, hearing it, Ryan's head came up sharply.

'So now you know—you've had your little triumph so you can go and——'

'I'm not going anywhere,' Anna put in quietly and saw his head go back in shock and bewilderment. 'I'm not leaving until I tell you something.'

'I don't want to hear——' Ryan began angrily, but Anna couldn't let him finish.

'I *loved* you', he had said, not 'I *love* you'. In the past he had cared, and now, like Rory, she was convinced he still did. But she had to get past his stubborn, hurt pride to make him admit it.

'I want to tell you where I've been,' she said, exerting every ounce of control possible to keep her voice calm and firm. She even made herself sit down and drive home the point that she intended to stay, and after a moment Ryan, with obvious reluctance, followed her lead. His face still had that stony, hostile expression, but at least he was listening.

'On Monday, after that meeting with Marc, I had a phone call. I've been looking for possible sites for new shops, and a contact had found what he thought was the perfect place in Nottingham. I arranged to drive up that afternoon and see it—and that was when I had an idea. If I had to drive north anyway—then why not go a bit further?'

She had Ryan's attention now, she could see it in the way those clear eyes were fixed on her face, but he didn't say a word, not even to encourage her to go on.

'I tried to ring you but couldn't get through so I left a message with Gillie. I didn't want to tell you exactly what I had planned—not until I'd actually done it; it was something I had to do on my own.'

The importance of what she was saying overcame her careful control, her voice rising in excitement.

'Ryan—I went to Forgeley. I went back and faced it all, looked my past squarely in the face—and it wasn't at all as I remember it. I'd forgotten there was that huge park so close to Empire Street—and the river, and that wonderful old wool hall with a room for every day of the year, where the weavers used to bring their cloth to sell. I'd forgotten how magnificent it was—or perhaps I never looked at it properly, as I didn't see so much else. I saw all the ugliness, but there was a lot of beauty too—beauty I was blind to.'

As she had been to Ryan, she thought sadly. If only she'd known how he'd felt then. But even if she had known, conditioned by her father, she would probably have behaved in exactly the same way, perhaps worse.

'I love the way they've turned the wool hall into all those little shops—it would be a fantastic place to have a Nature's Secrets outlet, and Marc thinks so too——'

'*Denton* was with you?' Ryan demanded harshly, and, fearful that she'd lost him again, Anna rushed on urgently.

'Only yesterday—on my last day there; I rang him to tell him about the hall and he came haring up to see for himself—you know Marc, he doesn't think anyone can do anything as well as he can. I—I took him all round Forgeley—I even showed him Empire Street.'

Suddenly Ryan's silence, apart from that one sharp question, became too much to bear. Turning towards him, her hands outstretched but not touching him because she knew he would not tolerate that yet, Anna willed him to understand.

'Ryan, I told him everything—where I grew up—how I'd lived—about my father——'

'And what did he think about that?'

It wasn't the reaction she wanted, but at least he was responding.

'He was angry at first—naturally; after all, I'd lied to him for nearly three years—and when he saw Empire Street he was shocked—and repelled.'

She'd seen that on his face, the appalled expression with which he had stared at the shabby, narrow street, the tone of his voice when he said, 'You lived *here*?'

'But, Ryan, don't you see? It didn't matter! Marc's reaction was everything I expected—everything I'd always dreaded—but I didn't care. I knew he could never really have loved me, because if he had my background wouldn't have mattered, and anyway I no longer worried about what he thought because all he is to me now is my business partner—and he's quite prepared to let things continue like that. After all, he knows that Nature's Secrets is a financially sound investment. But I wanted—I needed him to know the truth. So don't you see, Ryan? *Empire Street* was the unfinished business I still had to deal with, to get out of my system—not you.'

'Anna,' Ryan said slowly, and to her intense relief some of the attacking quality had gone out of his voice. 'I want to ask you one question—why did you go to Forgeley?'

It was the question she had been hoping and praying for since she had started her story, and Anna answered it directly and honestly.

'Because I had to face up to my past and get it into proportion once and for all—and because I wanted to see the place that meant so much to you—the place that will probably come to mean the same to me if—when—I go to live there...'

That got through to him, his blue eyes narrowing in a perplexed frown.

'When you—Anna, are you telling me that you're going to live in Yorkshire?'

'I hope so,' Anna responded sincerely. 'But that's up to you. I couldn't live there alone—but, with the man I love beside me, it would be a wonderful place to make my home.'

'The man——' Ryan shook his dark head in confusion. 'Just what are you trying to say?'

Anna knew that this was no time for half-measures—it was all or nothing.

'That I love you and I want to live with you—be your wife if that's what you want, have your children——'

Had she gone too far? Ryan's stunned expression, his silence worried her, but a moment later his face filled with a delight so overwhelming that it seemed the brightness of his eyes would blind her.

'If I—oh, Anna, it's what I want most in all the world!'

'Rory was right, then?'

'Rory was right.' Ryan's voice was deep and sincere. 'I love you—I think I always have, right from the moment when I first saw you as a thirteen-year-old. You knocked me off balance then, and I've never been right since. But whenever I tried to get close to you you froze me out.'

'I was afraid——'

'I know that now, but then I thought you were a snobbish little madam—but I still couldn't get you out of my mind. And of course when you fell for Larry I couldn't muscle in on my brother's territory.'

'But Larry never felt anything but friendship for me.'

She knew that now, knew that Larry had only been casually friendly, a much older brother to a loved younger sister—and perhaps that was what he had hoped for. Perhaps Larry had thought that if she kept coming round to see him then maybe one day she would realise how Ryan felt.

'Why didn't you tell me this on that night?' she asked, knowing there was no need to explain which night she meant.

'Tell you?' Ryan's tone was shaken and incredulous. 'Tell you that I loved you, when you called out my brother's name when *I* was making love to you?'

'Oh, Ryan, *no*!'

Anna's mind reeled at the thought of what she'd done, the pain she had unknowingly inflicted on him that night, on top of everything else he had been going through. She had thought him cold, callous, vicious, selfish; but instead he had been hurting far more than her—from the loss of his brother, the knowledge that his father thought him second best to Larry—and she had reinforced that feeling. She had thought that Larry's name had been only in her thoughts, but it seemed she had spoken it aloud and by doing so had devastated him so that he had turned on her savagely, like a wounded animal defending itself.

'Oh, Ryan—I'm so desperately sorry!'

'It's over——' A gesture from one long hand dismissed the past and its pain from their lives. 'And I hurt you too. When you ran away that night I cursed myself for being such an unfeeling brute. I tried everything I could to find you, but it seemed that you'd vanished off the face of the earth. I think, deep down, I've been looking for you ever since, and then, just when I'd given up, you come back into my life—and I set out to frighten you all over again!'

Ryan gave a wry, self-derisory laugh, shaking his head in disbelief.

'I never meant that blackmail threat. I was jealous as hell at the thought that you were going to marry someone else, especially someone like Denton. And I was angry too. I wasn't the Ryan Cassidy of eight years ago any more—I'd come a long way; to everyone else I was a success but it seemed that you still thought I wasn't good enough for you.'

'It wasn't that—it was more that I was afraid of what you'd tell Marc about me.'

'I came to see that.' Ryan's voice was soft. 'But before I did I was stunned to find that instead of wanting to get you and your snobbish prejudices out of my life I was prepared to try anything—even a bit of blackmail— to keep you coming to my flat, even if it was only to have your portrait painted. I was determined to do every damn thing I could to get you to change your mind about Marc Denton, and at least that way I could see you— talk to you——'

'Get me to fall in love with you.'

'I never hoped for that. It's more than I ever dreamed possible. Oh, Anna, my love, come here and let me hold you.'

Anna went into his arms willingly, lifting her face for his kiss, a wonderful glow of happiness suffusing her whole body.

'Did you mean what you said?' Ryan asked when at last their lips parted reluctantly. 'Would you really marry me and live in Yorkshire?'

'I'd live anywhere in the world with you,' Anna assured him.

'But your company—your job——'

'I was already thinking of ways to expand. Yorkshire—starting with the wool hall—seems to be the perfect place. I can employ a manager to deal with the shops here while I set up the northern end of things. You said yourself that you sometimes have to be in London, so I can keep an eye on everything down here too—we can combine the two bases quite easily.'

'I can't believe it—it's all too good to be true. Anna, if you only knew how much I love you—I want to love you for the rest of your life.'

'And when I'm sixty-five will you paint my portrait with all the lines of life on my face like the one you did of Mona?'

'You have my word on that,' Ryan assured her. 'And, like Mona, you'll grow more beautiful with every day that passes—and I'll be there to watch it happen.'

Anna surrendered to his embrace once more, feeling the fire of passion flare up in him as his hands moved over her body, setting her blood alight until she was suddenly jolted out of her reverie by Ryan's soft curse.

'Is there something wrong?'

'Nothing's *wrong*.' Ryan's voice was husky with an echo of the desire that flooded Anna's veins. 'It's just that Maeve and Rory won't stay out all day—and what I want most in all the world is to be able to take you to bed and show you how much I love you.'

'Ah, well——' Anna's smile was teasing, sensually inviting '—I think you've underestimated your sister-in-law there. Judging by the look on her face, I should imagine that she was determined to stay out of the flat for some considerable time.'

'Long enough?' Ryan queried, a gleam in his blue eyes.

'Quite long enough,' Anna said firmly. 'But not if we waste much more time talking.'

'I have no intention of wasting *any* time at all,' Ryan assured her, swinging her up into his arms and carrying her towards his bedroom.

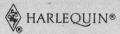

1993

The most romantic day of the year is here! Escape into the exquisite
world of love with MY VALENTINE 1993. What better way to celebrate
Valentine's Day than with this very romantic, sensuous collection of four
original short stories, written by some of Harlequin's most popular
authors.

**ANNE STUART
JUDITH ARNOLD
ANNE McALLISTER
LINDA RANDALL WISDOM**

**THIS VALENTINE'S DAY, DISCOVER ROMANCE
WITH MY VALENTINE 1993**

Available in February wherever Harlequin Books are sold.   VAL93

COME FOR A VISIT—TEXAS-STYLE!

Where do you find hot Texas nights, smooth Texas charm and dangerously sexy cowboys? CRYSTAL CREEK!

This March, join us for a year in Crystal Creek...where power and influence live in the land, and in the hands of one family determined to nourish old Texas fortunes and to forge new Texas futures.

CRYSTAL CREEK reverberates with the exciting rhythm of Texas. Each story features the rugged individuals who live and love in the Lone Star State. And each one ends with the same invitation...

Y'ALL COME BACK...REAL SOON!

Watch for this exciting saga of a unique Texas family in March, wherever Harlequin Books are sold.

CC-G

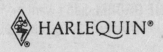

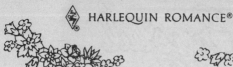

HARLEQUIN ROMANCE®

**Harlequin Romance
takes you to Alaska
for a wedding!**

Join us there
when you read
next month's title in

THE BRIDAL COLLECTION

**A BRIDE FOR RANSOM (#3251)
by Renee Roszel**

THE BRIDE wasn't looking for a husband.
THE GROOM didn't want a wife.
BUT THE WEDDING was right for both of them!

Available this month in
The Bridal Collection:
**SHOWDOWN!
by Ruth Jean Dale
Harlequin Romance #3242**